CATHY'S LITTLE SISTER

CATHY'S
LITTLE
SISTER

CATHERINE WOOLLEY

ILLUSTRATED BY
LIZ DAUBER

WILLIAM MORROW AND COMPANY
NEW YORK

CONTENTS

CATHY'S LITTLE SISTER

CHAPTER ONE
CATHY STAYS HOME

Chris watched from a bedroom window as the yellow school bus pulled away from the foot of the Leonards' driveway. Her sister's best friend, Naomi Hughes, had climbed on the bus as usual, but Cathy herself was not going to school this morning. Cathy was right here in her room, dressed, but lying on the bed.

Chris turned from the window. "The bus is gone."

"Was Naomi on it?" Cathy asked.

"Yes."

Cathy turned impatiently on the bed. "I'm just furious that I have to be sick and stay home! This is the day I write up school news for the paper."

Chris regarded her older sister. It seemed

strange to see her lying here, looking wan. Cathy practically never missed school because of illness or for any other reason. She loved school and had many projects there that urgently required her attention at all times.

Chris suddenly thought how nice it would be if she could spend the day with Cathy.

"Are you ready for school, Chris?" Mother called up the stairs. "Jeff has gone."

"Almost," Chris called back. "Cathy," she said, "I wish I could stay home."

Chris and seven-year-old Jeff did not travel by bus. They attended the Middle Bridge School, which housed the first four grades.

"Well, you can't," Cathy informed her from the bed. "Would you please open the window, Chris. And Mother told you to hurry."

Chris pushed up the window, and the cool, sunny air of the spring day floated in. Out on the broad front lawn of the Leonard house the great trees and bushes were just beginning to come into bud, and here and there a glimmer of green showed in the brown winter grass. As Chris lingered, looking out, a fat robin alighted from nowhere.

"Chris, if you aren't dressed, get dressed this minute," Mother called.

She went slowly into her own room and reluctantly began to climb into her clothes, muttering. "I don't see why I can't stay home just this one day." She put on her long-sleeved sweater as she talked to herself, found a pleated skirt, and slipped it over her head. She zipped up the skirt and sat down to draw on socks and shoes, giving an annoyed snap to the shoelaces. Then she ran a comb through her soft locks.

She was going through the bathroom between her room and Cathy's when Mother called once more. "You are going to be late if you don't start right now!"

Further delay was going to serve no purpose. Chris called good-by to Cathy and went downstairs. She spoke to her parakeet in the library, picked up her books, and went through the dining room to the kitchen. Mother had just finished the dishes, and Mr. Pickle, the mother cat, with her current offspring Fluff snuggled close, lay stretched out in a patch of sunshine. Chris picked up Fluff, warm and purring.

"Hurry along," Mother said.

Chris bent her cheek to Fluff's velvet coat. "Is Cathy very sick?"

"She may be coming down with a cold or a little virus. I'll take care of Cathy. Here's an apple for recess." Mother put the shiny red apple in her hand, kissed Chris's cheek, and turned her firmly toward the door. "Now *will* you be off?"

Even now, Chris did not hurry. She liked school well enough, but it was hard to put distance between herself and home, with Cathy there. It was not until she came in sight of the school playground and saw that the pupils had gone in, that she felt a stir of alarm and began to run. When she had reached the school, climbed to the second floor, and opened the door of the classroom, she was breathless.

Heads turned as she came in, and two of the girls, Janice Newton and Emily Page, put their hands over their mouths in expressions of shocked disapproval.

Mrs. Franz looked up. "You're quite late, Chris." Before Chris could answer, she added, "Speak to me later, please. Here's the paper for your arithmetic."

Chris's spirits were already low. They dived

lower still. She loved and greatly admired Mrs. Franz, with her kind, deeply lined face and iron-gray hair. She was crushed to have her teacher address her in a cold, unfriendly fashion.

After arithmetic the class broke up into groups to work on scenes from a book, which they were making into a P.T.A. play. The play was a tradition of Middle Bridge School. Every year the four grades collaborated to produce a drama, which they presented at an evening meeting of the Parent-Teacher Association. All the mothers and fathers came. Refreshments were served, and altogether it was a great night, a big thing to look forward to. Fourth graders did much of the work and played the leading roles, so this year Chris's class was very busy. The adaptation of scenes from the book was almost complete.

Chris obediently went up to Mrs. Franz before recess. "What happened, Chris? You're always on time," Mrs. Franz said.

"Well, Cathy is sick and stayed home from school, and I was sort of taking care of her."

"I'm sorry Cathy isn't feeling well."

"It's just a cold or a virus."

"Well, don't you catch it. All right, Chris."

She felt happier. Eating her apple, she went skipping outside, where Janice joined her. "Chris," Janice said, "know what I was thinking? Your hair is light and mine's dark, just like those two girls in our play. Let's ask Mrs. Franz if we can play the parts of those girls."

Chris set her teeth in the juicy flesh of the apple. She had given no thought to having a part in the play, but now that she had squared herself with Mrs. Franz she was feeling agreeable to anything. "O.K.," she said.

"Oh, good! We'll have fun. Could you bring your lunch some days, so we can learn our parts together?"

"I guess so." She and Jeff usually went home to have lunch with Mother.

"Chris." Janice took small bites out of a big yellow apple. "Have you got a best friend?"

Chris considered, munching. Middle Bridge was a mere four corners of a village, and most of the pupils came to school by bus from other small towns, set in the surrounding farmland and dairy country of New Jersey. As it happened, not a single girl in her class lived here in the village. This meant the other girls went home from school on the bus, and there was no opportunity for Chris to play with any of them except on the school ground. She had no real friendships in school. She did not miss them, however, because she had Cathy and Jeff.

"My sister's my best friend," she said.

"*Sisters* can't be best friends!"

"Why not?"

"Because they're *sisters,* and in different grades. Best friends have to be in the same grade. Chris, we can be best friends, if you want to, just like those girls in the book."

Emily came running up to them just then, jump rope in hand. "Chris and Janice, want to play jump rope?" The conversation about best friends broke off.

As she absent-mindedly turned the rope for Emily to jump, Chris thought over what Janice had said. She was not averse to having a best friend. It just didn't seem important. She glanced in the direction of home. From here she could almost see the big white house with its broad grounds and the old orchard out back. She could get just a glimpse of the little new house, close by the big old-fashioned one, where Naomi and her widowed mother lived.

She tried to picture what Cathy was doing now.

Was she asleep, or sitting up having some orange juice? If she wasn't very sick, they could have been having a lovely time together today. What a shame she had felt fine herself and had to come to school.

And into her mind drifted the warning Mrs. Franz had issued. "Don't you catch it," the teacher had said.

Until this moment Chris had indeed felt in perfect health. Now, all of a sudden, it seemed to her she had a lump in her throat. She swallowed hard. Then she sniffed. Was she getting a sniffle? Chris gave a small cough. She certainly did feel as if she were getting a cold.

The rest of the morning she experimented, swallowing, sniffing, and coughing dry little coughs. By lunchtime she had convinced herself she was coming down with something. After all, what could be more natural than that she should have what Cathy had?

Of course, if she was sick, she would have to stay home this afternoon. Mother would insist on that. Cathy hadn't even wanted to stay home and Mother had said she must.

Usually Chris walked home with Jeff, but this noon she was in a hurry and didn't look for her brother. She jogged steadily along the path through the fields, and reached home warm, flushed, and breathless.

Mother was putting their lunch on the table as she came in.

"Hello, dear."

"Hi," Chris said, panting. "Mother, I think I'm coming down with what Cathy's got."

"Do you think so?" Mother looked concerned and put a hand on her forehead. "You feel a little warm."

"I am." Chris neglected to mention that she had run all the way. "And I keep coughing." She demonstrated. "I think I'd better stay home this afternoon."

"Well, if you're sick. Have your lunch and we'll see."

"I want to go upstairs first. Just a minute," Chris said.

Excitedly, positive now that she didn't feel a bit well, she trotted through the house and ran upstairs. She went into Cathy's room—and stopped short. The bed was neatly made. The room was empty.

"Cathy?" Chris went into her mother's room,

the other bedrooms, even the bathrooms. She went back downstairs, where Jeff and Mother were eating. "Where's Cathy?"

"Cathy woke up and felt fine and wanted to go to school. So I took her."

Chris stood, speechless.

"Sit down and eat your chicken soup," Mother said. "Your stomach isn't upset, is it?"

She couldn't believe fate had played this trick upon her. "What? No, my stomach's all right. It isn't fair!" Chris burst out in spite of herself.

"What isn't fair?"

"I thought Cathy would be home!"

Mother looked at her and raised her eyebrows. "Oh, so that's it. Well, maybe you'll feel better, too, after you've had your lunch."

Too disgusted with the turn of events to reply, Chris slid into her seat and shook out her napkin.

They finished their lunch, and Jeff went off to find his friend Mike and play ball. "Whether you're sick or not," Mother said, looking at Chris keenly, "you look a little worked up to me. Go and lie down for ten minutes."

"I'm not *very* sick." She hated to admit that just possibly she had conjured up her illness but,

after all, if Cathy wasn't going to be here, she might as well go back to school.

"Rest for a few minutes, anyway."

Perhaps she was tired from the strain of producing symptoms or from disappointment, but Chris fell asleep at once on the living-room sofa. When she opened her eyes, Mr. Pickle lay curled against her and Mother was standing there.

"How do you feel?"

"Fine." Chris raised herself on her elbow. "What time is it?"

"A quarter of two."

It was too late to go to school now. She swung her legs off the sofa and sat blinking.

"I called the school," Mother said. She felt Chris's head again. "You feel cool now, but a quiet afternoon won't hurt you."

It hadn't worked out at all as she had expected. And now she had an afternoon to kill before Cathy and Jeff got home. "What can I do?" she asked gloomily.

"Well, do you feel like making some of those cookies that you and Cathy like? We're all out of homemade cookies."

"I guess so."

She changed into dungarees and went down to the kitchen. "What do I do first?"

"Look up the recipe." Mother handed her a cookbook.

"But Cathy always looks it up. I don't know. . . ."

"They're called sugar-drop cookies. Just look in the index. I think it would be very nice if you made these by yourself," Mother said. "I'll be here if you need me."

Chris had never made cookies by herself, and she felt quite at sea. She finally found the recipe, read it through, and wandered about the kitchen collecting utensils. But nothing seemed to go as smoothly as when Cathy was in charge. Sugar and butter refused to blend, making hard lumps which would not squash. The egg, which always cracked and broke so neatly for Cathy, got bits of shell in it. When she transferred flour from canister to sifter, she spilled it on the floor, and she forgot to sift the salt and baking soda with the flour.

Finally she called for help. "I can't get it a bit smooth!"

Mother beat the lumpy batter for her. "Now

I'll light the oven, and you drop the batter on the cookie sheet."

Chris was putting messy spoonfuls on the sheet, when Mother said, "Did you grease the sheet?"

She hadn't. She tried to scrape the batter off and made a botch of it. Chris sighed loudly.

"Honey, you and Cathy make these all the time," Mother protested.

"I know, but Cathy always does most of it. And she tells me everything to do."

She got a sheet of cookies in the oven at last, however, and sat down at the kitchen table to wait for them to bake, while Mother moved about putting the flour and butter and eggs away. Chris glanced at the clock. Cathy would soon be home now.

She thought of her conversation with Janice. "Mother," she said, "I haven't got a best friend, have I?"

"You will have." Mother was sweeping up the flour. "There just doesn't happen to be anyone your age around here right now."

Chris considered. "Cathy's really my best friend. But I'm not her best friend. She likes Naomi better."

"Cathy loves you dearly!" Mother told her. "You're her little sister. But Naomi is the same age and in the same class, and they have a lot in common, that's all." She glanced at Chris's serious little face. "You'll have lots of friends, dear, don't be worried."

"I'm not." Chris relaxed. "A girl in my class, Janice, said she'd be my best friend. And we're going to ask Mrs. Franz if we can play the parts of best friends in the play."

"Good. Well, there you are. . . . Chris, your cookies!" Mother exclaimed.

Chris scrambled up, grabbing a pot holder, but she was a little too late. When she drew out the sheet the cookies were black around the edges.

"I'm going in the other room and let you concentrate," said Mother.

Chris protested. She couldn't do it alone! But Mother deserted her, so she laboriously scraped the sheet and dropped more cookies onto it. She planted her chair in front of the range and kept peeking in the oven. And at last she drew out a sheet of cookies, a little higgledy-piggledy perhaps, but unburned.

Finally the last cookies were out. If some were

unbecomingly dark, or a few unattractively pallid, they looked beautiful to Chris. She gazed at the result of her efforts, and called Mother to admire.

"Cathy'll be surprised," Chris remarked with satisfaction. She could hardly wait for Cathy to get home. She broke off a piece of cookie and ate it. It really was good, almost as good, she decided, as Cathy's cookies. She held a crumb down for Mr. Pickle, but the dignified cat sniffed delicately, switched her tail in disdain, and stalked away.

Jeff arrived, stamping in at the back door, pink-cheeked and starving. "Oh boy, cookies!" He scooped up a handful.

Chris shielded the rest. "Don't eat too many, Jeff! I want to show Cathy." Jeff was already on his way out to play ball.

Then Cathy was home, coming in the front door like a spring breeze, and singing out, "What do I smell?" as she traipsed through into the kitchen with her armful of books.

Chris stood expectantly, her eyes shining. Cathy stopped in the doorway. "What's going on around here?"

"I stayed home this afternoon," Chris cried. "And look at the cookies I made, Cathy! All by myself." She glanced at Mother. "Almost all by myself."

"What in the world did you stay home for?"

Chris hesitated, and Mother helped her out. "She thought she was coming down with something, just like you this morning."

"Oh. And are you?"

"What?" Chris asked.

"Coming down with something?"

"Oh, no."

"That's good." Cathy deposited her books on the table and picked up a cookie. "These are quite good, Chris—considering you made them," she added with a chuckle. She started for the back door, cookie in hand. "I'm going over to Naomi's."

"I'm going too," Chris cried. After all, she had been waiting all afternoon for Cathy to come home.

But her sister shook her head. "No, Chris, Naomi and I have something very important that we have to discuss."

"What is it?"

Cathy had the back door open and was halfway out. "I may tell you tomorrow," she threw over her shoulder. "We have to discuss it privately first. By now."

She pulled the door shut behind her, and was gone, leaving Chris and her brave array of cookies behind.

CHAPTER TWO

A RAINY NIGHT

Chris was up early next morning. This was a new day, and she willingly put yesterday behind her. The sun held warmth this morning; the dew-drenched grass flashed rainbow colors. As she let the screen door bang behind her and followed Cathy across the yard to Naomi's house, Chris's nose crinkled to greet the smells of spring.

Naomi opened the door as they approached. "Hi."

"Hi," Cathy said. "It's time for the bus. We'd better hurry."

Naomi snatched up her books, called good-by to her mother, and the girls started down the drive, Chris trailing behind. "Cathy, did you ask your mother?" Naomi said as they walked along.

"Not yet," Cathy replied. "But I was thinking

about whom to invite, and you know what? I think I'll ask my friend Judy, back where we lived before we came to Middle Bridge."

"Then I'll ask Patty Ellsworth. She's my friend in New York," Naomi cried.

"Invite them to what?" Chris inquired, coming abreast.

The girls exchanged looks. "I wasn't going to tell you yet," Cathy said, "but I will. I'm going to have a slumber party—if Mother'll let me."

"Naomi!" They all turned at the sound of Mrs. Hughes' voice. "You left your lunch."

"Oh, I forgot it." Naomi started back up the drive.

"There's the bus!" Chris cried.

"Oh, Chris, please run and hold it," Cathy exclaimed. "You can run faster than I can."

Obediently Chris's legs flew, and she reached the road as the school bus drew to a stop. "They're coming," she told the driver. "Wait. Here they come!"

Cathy and Naomi were racing down the drive. "Thanks, Chrissy," they both gasped, pulling themselves up on the step. Chris watched the bus off, then turned toward her own school.

Her mind busied itself with thoughts of a

slumber party. How exciting it sounded! As she approached the playground she looked forward to finding Janice there and telling her they were going to have a slumber party at her house.

She spied Janice bouncing a ball on the far side of the playground. Chris ran eagerly to join her. "Janice!" she called. "Hi, Janice!"

Janice looked up, but instead of coming to meet Chris she suddenly turned deliberately and ran the other way.

Chris stopped, uncertain. What in the world? She advanced more slowly. Janice had stopped and was bouncing her ball furiously, her back to Chris.

"Hi, Janice," Chris said cautiously.

"I don't want to speak to you." Janice kept her eyes on her ball.

"Why not?" Chris cried.

"You know why."

"I don't."

"Well!" Janice kept on bouncing, but she turned slightly, as if by accident, toward Chris. "I said we could ask Mrs. Franz to let you and me play those girls in the play, and you said O.K."

"I know."

"Then you stayed home yesterday afternoon!" Janice cried.

"But I was. . . . I didn't feel well and my mother made me stay. What's that got to do with the play?"

"Mrs. Franz gave out the parts. Emily's going to play the other girl."

Chris was shocked. Until this moment she had not known that she wanted to be in the play. Now suddenly she realized that since yesterday she had been looking forward to it. She gave a little moan of dismay.

The bell rang. Without another glance Janice started for the building, Chris tagging miserably behind.

The cast was to start rehearsals that afternoon. Mrs. Franz spoke to Chris. "We had to get started, Chris. How would you like to be in charge of properties?"

Chris looked uncertain.

"Properties are the things we use on the stage. We need a couple of chairs and a table, and we need a hammock for the second act. Do you have a hammock with a stand at home?"

"No."

"Perhaps you can find one. We'll make you properties chairman then, Chris."

It wasn't as much fun as having a part in the play, and she had no idea where to look for a hammock. But Cathy would know. Cathy was very smart at anything like that.

Well, I don't care if I'm not going to be in the play, Chris told herself. We're going to have a slumber party, and that's just as much fun. Her mind busied itself with the slumber party all morning.

As she went home at noon, she noticed that Janice and Emily were going off with their arms around each other to eat lunch and study their parts. Apparently Emily was to be Janice's best friend now. I don't care, Chris told herself again.

She said to Mother as they were having lunch, "Cathy's going to have a slumber party."

"Is she indeed?" Mother raised her eyebrows.

"Yes. She's going to invite Naomi and Judy and a friend of Naomi's."

"Let's hear about it from Cathy," Mother suggested.

The cast held its first rehearsal for the play that afternoon and, as properties chairman, Chris could have stayed to watch. But she couldn't get home fast enough to hear the plans for the slumber party. She met Cathy at the front door.

"I told Mother about the slumber party!" she cried.

Cathy's eyes flew to her mother. "Oh, may I have it?"

"I shouldn't wonder," said Mother.

"Oh, you darling mother!" They trooped into the kitchen, and Cathy poured herself some milk.

"May I invite someone too?" Chris asked suddenly.

"No!" Cathy cried. "This is my party, Chris!"

Chris sat silent for a moment. "I can't think of anybody to invite, anyway. I don't know anyone from away."

Jeff came in, puffing and rosy. "Chris, come out on the front porch. A bird's building a nest."

She got slowly to her feet to follow him, torn between wanting to hear more about the party and wanting to see the nest. As she went into the dining room she heard Cathy say in a low voice, "Mother, if Patty and Judy can come, may I invite some girls in our class—like Martha and Gretchen—too? And could the children—Chris and Jeff—please eat dinner in the kitchen that night?"

Chris popped back. "Do I have to?" she cried, in a piteous appeal to her mother.

Mother looked at her, then at Cathy. Cathy

flushed slightly. "I didn't mean to hurt your feelings, Chris. But if you eat with us, Jeff will want to. I'd like a nice grown-up dinner!" she added wistfully. "Jeff will tip something over!"

"But it's simply horrible to eat in the kitchen with Jeff!"

"Chris," Mother said, "this is Cathy's party. Some time you'll have a party and Cathy won't be invited. Go along and see the bird's nest now."

She went, unhappily. She was in the backyard with Jeff when Cathy came out, heading for Naomi's. "Chris won't play with me," Jeff complained.

"I didn't say I wouldn't," Chris corrected. Actually she was too disturbed to feel like racing around as she usually did with Jeff, too upset at the prospect of being relegated to the kitchen. She had been so thrilled with the idea of the party.

"She'll play with you, Jeff," Cathy said reassuringly, and went on to Naomi's.

Chris stood looking after her. She's going to tell Naomi that she can have the party, she thought. They're going to talk about it. "Why don't you go over to Mike's?" she suggested to her brother.

When Jeff had gone off, disgusted with her for

not wanting to play with him, Chris wandered around aimlessly. Finally she could not stand being left out a minute longer, and she sauntered casually to Naomi's door and rang the bell. Through the window she could see the two girls settled at the table, though they did not seem to be deeply involved with school books.

Mrs. Hughes opened the door. "Hello, Chris."

Chris stepped inside, as Cathy glanced up. "I just came to ask if Whiskers can come out," she announced. She could not keep from gazing longingly in the direction of the two older girls.

"Why, I suppose Whiskers can go out," Mrs. Hughes said. "He's asleep on my bed." But Chris, having gained entry, was advancing slowly across the room.

"We're doing homework," Cathy informed her.

"I know." They were really talking about the slumber party, Chris was sure.

Mrs. Hughes brought Whiskers, blinking sleepily, from the bedroom. "Here's our kitty." Chris accepted him from her arms.

"Why don't you play with Fluff?" Cathy demanded.

"Because I'd rather have Whiskers today." Chris

moved toward the door with seeming dignity, but with lagging feet.

"By now, dear," Mrs. Hughes said.

"By." But Chris could not make her voice sound happy. She wanted so much to stay and hear the slumber-party talk.

Five minutes later she saw the strange dog. He was a big dog, and he was out in the orchard, looking in her direction, tail waving tentatively. Chris loved dogs. She had to make the acquaintance of this one. She rang Naomi's bell again.

"I brought him back," she said, handing the cat over to Mrs. Hughes, "because I saw a dog and I thought it wouldn't be safe."

She was heading for the orchard when she heard Cathy open the door and shout, "Chris, be careful. That's a strange dog and you don't know him."

But Chris and the dog had already met, and from the frisking and tail wagging that went on Chris was quite certain this was no dangerous beast.

That night at dinner she had momentarily forgotten the slumber party and her grievance concerning it. "Daddy, this big dog was here," she related. "And he just loves to play, and he caught sticks when I threw them, and he brought them right back to me!"

"I wonder if he's the one that's been keeping your mother and me awake half the night," Daddy remarked.

"Oh, no!" Chris said hastily.

But that night, perhaps because Daddy had mentioned the barking dog, Chris heard him too. The barking went on for a long time, fading and swelling as the dog galloped about.

Chris did not lie awake long, but Mother and Daddy were kept from sleep by the barking for the next two nights. Finally, at breakfast, Daddy said, "We can't stand this any longer. We'll have to call the state police and have them pick him up."

"Oh!" Chris cried, anguished.

"He's a stray," Mother reminded her. "He may be lost and some little child may be looking for him."

"Well, I hope they don't catch him, so there!" Chris went off to school deeply troubled.

When she came home that afternoon, there was a state trooper's car in front of the house. Chris stood miserably in the living room between the officer and her mother.

"We'll set a box trap out back, Mrs. Leonard," the trooper was saying.

"A trap!" Chris cried in horror.

"It won't hurt him," the officer explained. "He'll just go in to get the food and the door will drop. Then we'll pick him up."

Cathy came home then, and the girls went along as the trooper took the trap from his car and set it in the backyard. "Have you got something we can bait this with?" he asked.

"No," Chris said promptly.

"Will cat food do?" asked Cathy.

"If he's hungry he'll go for anything."

Cathy brought the can of cat food, and the officer baited the trap. "Now we'll see if we have a dog by morning."

Chris awoke in the night to hear the dog barking, but she drifted off again. Early in the morning she opened her eyes, and was suddenly wide awake. The dog, she thought. She had to go out and see whether her friend was in the trap.

She was almost dressed when she heard Cathy stirring. Cathy came through their bathroom to her door. "Are you going out to see about the dog?" she inquired. "Wait for me, I'm getting dressed."

They went downstairs together and out into the flushed dawn. And in the trap they beheld not the dog—but Mr. Pickle. Mr. Pickle, furious, her tail twice its normal size. Mr. Pickle, who liked cat food very much and had taken the practical measure, while awaiting rescue, of gobbling the bait.

Chris and Cathy stood there, laughing aloud in their relief. "Oh, poor Mr. Pickle!" Cathy cried. "We didn't mean to. Here, we'll let you out."

Chris tried to catch the indignant puss as Cathy raised the door, but Mr. Pickle eluded her and was out like a streak. Once beyond reach, she slowed her pace to a dignified stroll, shook herself free of the night's degrading experience, and departed without a backward look.

"She's mad," Chris remarked.

"Simply seething," Cathy agreed, and they ran in, laughing.

Chris hoped that this would end the dog catching, but she hoped in vain. They trapped the dog the next night. Unlike Mr. Pickle, however, the dog harbored no ill will about his cramped quarters and no resentment against those responsible. He greeted Chris and Cathy with an ecstatic wagging of his tail. Chris wanted to let him out.

"No, Chris!" Cathy cried. "You forgot the state trooper is going to take him away in the trap."

"He's not!" Chris said. "I'm going to ask Mother if I can keep him."

Mother, hurrying to get breakfast, was not in a receptive mood. "Chris, he barks all night. Besides, we have Mr. Pickle and Fluff, a parakeet, and a slumber party coming up."

"But *I* haven't got a slumber party coming up." Chris turned away, the corners of her mouth trembling. "And I can't be in the play, or *anything*."

Cathy was putting bread in the toaster. Mother looked at Chris in surprise. "I thought you said you were going to be in the play."

It had slipped out. Chris had not mentioned this before, because she didn't want anyone to know about her disappointment or the trouble with Janice. She stood there now, silent.

Mother asked no questions. "Come here, dear." Chris came, eyes glistening suspiciously. "I know how you love the dog. But I don't see how we can keep another pet, especially one that barks all night."

Chris sniffed up tears. "Maybe he won't if I feed him."

"Maybe not." Mother gave a sigh as she transferred bacon to a hot plate. "Well, Chris, suppose you give him something to eat today, and we'll see what happens tonight. But if he keeps on barking, will you be reasonable?"

Chris nodded and looked up. "Can I let him out now?"

"Eat your breakfast first. He's all right."

The toast popped up, and Chris took a piece and buttered it, suddenly happy again. "I'm glad the dog can stay, Chrissy," Cathy told her.

Chris nodded. "Yes, because you have a slumber party to look forward to. Now I at least have a dog. I'm going to name him Rover," she decided.

Mother bought some dog food, and after school Chris fed the animal, who wolfed down his meal in two gulps. There was a night of peace. Then Chris awoke to a rainy day. By the time she came home from school the rain had turned into fog. The dog showed up to be fed, but she could not go out and play with him. That evening she went to the window several times, wondering where he would spend this miserable night.

Cathy read her mind and came to look over her shoulder. "Do you see him anywhere?" Chris shook her head.

It was some time in the night when Chris awoke and came slowly to full consciousness under her warm blankets. She could hear rain again, a relentless downpour. And out in the rain somewhere, soaked and shivering, was Rover.

She stood it as long as she could. Then she softly got out of bed and found her slippers. The door squeaked slightly as she went out into the hall. Moving cautiously, so the steps wouldn't creak, she crept downstairs.

He was somewhere close by, and when she opened the back door he came up the steps and into the kitchen, one wild soaked scamper, leaping upon her with joy. Chris tried to quiet him. "Sh! Oh, you're soaked!" She got a dish towel and mopped him. "I won't make you go out in this rain again, so there! You can go in the cellar."

He had no intention of going to the cellar. When she held the door open, he stood in the middle of the floor, wet and bedraggled, cocked his head, and dared her. Chris shut the door. Well, she had tried, and she couldn't help it if he wouldn't go down. "Then you'll have to come up in my room," she told him.

He climbed the stairs with her silently enough, and she softly shut her bedroom door behind them,

drawing a breath of relief. "Now lie down on the floor," she whispered.

He settled himself, though his eyes, questioning her, were bright. Chris got into bed herself, turned out the light, and snuggled into the bedclothes. There were soft stirrings as the dog arranged himself comfortably, and Chris listened tensely. But soon he seemed quiet, and she began to relax.

She was almost asleep when a loud and ringing bark broke the silence. Chris's eyes flew open and she sat up, reaching for the switch on the lamp beside her bed. "Be quiet!" she ordered. When the light went on he was at the door, telling her clearly that he had important concerns elsewhere, rain or no rain.

The damage was done now. Voices arose in her parents' room. Lights went on. In a minute the door opened and Daddy came in.

"Chris, what are you up to and what is this dog doing here?" he said sternly.

"I wiped him off," Chris said quickly.

"Who gave you permission to bring him into the house?"

"Nobody. But, Daddy, you wouldn't want to be a dog and have to stay out in this pouring rain!"

Chris was sitting up, distressed, while the dog waved his tail tentatively and looked from one to the other. Rain pelted the windows. In the bathroom Cathy, also aroused, was getting a drink. The thought slid through Chris's mind that Cathy was going to be tactful, and not embarrass her by coming in.

"Well, I wouldn't, at that," Daddy said after a moment, gazing down at the animal. "It's teeming. I'll put him in the cellar this once, and we'll talk about it tomorrow."

She sighed with relief. "He wouldn't go down for me, but you can make him."

"Good night—you animal tamer." Daddy bent down to kiss her. "Come on, you beast." The dog galloped gaily after him, and after a minute Chris turned out her light. She heard her father come back, and the house grew still again.

But she could not go to sleep. Twice she got up for a drink of water, went back to bed, and tossed restlessly. They would probably take the dog away now, she told herself, lying there, the dog she had come to love. In the blackness of night she added this to her list of troubles.

After the third trip for a drink she lay awake, and when her door opened she turned wide eyes.

"Chris," Mother said in a low voice, "can't you go to sleep?"

"No."

Mother sat down on the edge of the bed and brushed the hair back from Chris's forehead. "Would you like a cup of cocoa?"

"Can I come downstairs and drink it?"

"Come on."

Hand in hand they went downstairs and through the house into the big warm kitchen, with its faint clean aroma of soapsuds from the dinner dishes. Mother snapped on the light. Mr. Pickle, invisible when the dog was there, blinked sleepily from her box, and Fluff climbed out, stretching his small paws. Chris got out crackers while Mother mixed sugar and cocoa and heated milk. The cocoa steamed fragrantly. They sat at the table.

"Mother," Chris said mournfully, "I don't think it's fair. I can't be in the slumber party or the play. And I haven't got a best friend, except Cathy, and Naomi's her best friend. And now I can't even have a dog friend!"

"You haven't lost your dog friend yet. I thought you said Janice was going to be your best friend."

"Now she isn't. She and Emily are in the play, and they're learning their parts together, and they're *always* together."

"Well." Mother reached for her hand, and changed the subject. "Your birthday comes during Easter week. Would you like to have a party?"

Chris considered, then shook her head. At the moment she didn't have the heart to plan a party. "No, because Janice is mad at me and she might not come, and then Emily wouldn't come. . . ." She took another sip of the warm, comforting drink, and sighed resignedly. "I'll just have my favorite food for dinner on my birthday, the way we always do."

Mother sat silent for a few moments. "We'll think of something special to do during Easter vacation. You think about what you would like to do, dear, and we'll plan it. And don't worry about Rover. He can stay for now, anyway."

CHAPTER THREE
GOOD NIGHT, CHRIS!

Each day now, as Chris came home from school, the Leonard lawn looked greener and more lush. The trees were throwing a lacework of leaves against the sky, white and purple crocuses showed their colors, and the fruit trees were pink with the rising sap.

Almost every afternoon the cast of the play stayed to rehearse. Chris usually stayed too, to watch. She had nothing to hurry home for. If her thoughts sometimes strayed to Cathy and Naomi, planning the slumber party, she told herself that even if she went home they would not share their plans with her. Cathy intended her to have no part in the party.

She had found chairs and a table for the play, but she had done nothing about locating a hammock. She was waiting for a good time to ask Cathy to help her.

Before Janice had brought up the subject of best friends Chris had felt no need of one, but now the intimacy between Janice and Emily made her an outsider. It was hard. At home there were Cathy and Naomi, always together talking about the slumber party. At school, Emily and Janice, rehearsing their parts together at recess and at lunchtime. Chris was left out of both projects.

Three of the guests had accepted Cathy's invitation. Chris detoured one day, coming home, to

buy an ice-cream cone. She was coming out of the store when Cathy dropped off the school bus at the post office next door. Licking around the edge of her chocolate cone, Chris followed her inside.

Cathy had a letter. "Good!" she said softly, skimming the page.

"Is it from Judy? Can she come?" Chris's teeth bit into the crisp cone.

"Yes. Come on, Chris, I'm in a hurry."

In the kitchen Chris listened while Cathy read Judy's acceptance to Mother. Cathy slipped the letter into the envelope with a sigh of satisfaction. "I'm going out and tell Naomi."

Chris trailed after her. "Cathy, I want to ask you something."

"What?"

"I'm in charge of properties for the play, and we have to have a hammock. But I don't know where one is."

"Well, I certainly don't."

"Will you help me find one?"

Cathy sighed, impatient to be on her way. "Why don't you go around and ask a few people?"

"Will you go with me?"

"I suppose so. If I ever have time."

"I want to ask you something else," Chris hurried on. "Mother said I could do something special during Easter week. Can you suggest something I can do?"

"Why don't you go to Radio City? That's what I'd do, Chrissy." Cathy was off to Naomi's.

Chris stood looking after her as Cathy knocked lightly and went in. With bitter envy she longed to be in there too, to hear the exciting plans, even if Cathy was not inviting her. She struggled for a while, then went and rang the bell.

Naomi came to the door. "I said that was you, Chris," Cathy remarked from the table.

"I came to see Mrs. Hughes."

Naomi looked toward the bedroom, and her mother's voice called, "Come on in, Chris."

Chris went into Mrs. Hughes' room. "Mrs. Hughes, my mother says I can have some special treat during Easter vacation. Can you suggest some special treat I can have?"

"Why don't you go to a museum in New York?"

Middle Bridge was an hour's trip from New York, but Chris seldom got there. "What's a museum like?" she asked.

"It's a big building where they have dinosaurs and birds and animals."

"Like the zoo?"

"No, these animals are dead."

"Oh, I remember. Jeff went there with Grandma." Personally, Chris preferred her animals alive.

She went into the living room and suddenly decided to abandon her pretense for coming in. "Naomi, could you and Cathy come out and play with me?"

"Chris," Cathy said, "we're studying."

"Then can I study here too?"

In the end she ran home for her books, and they made room for her. Chris was happy as she slipped into her chair, and as she glanced up and caught Cathy's eye her sister smiled at her. She reached over and patted Chris's shoulder. "You're a nice girl, Chrissy, even if you are a pest sometimes."

But she didn't sound as if she meant it—about being a pest. Chris wiggled like a pleased puppy.

They all worked seriously for a while. "There, that's all I'm going to do now," Cathy exclaimed, throwing down her pencil.

"I'm through, too," said Naomi.

Chris closed her own book quickly. "I'll finish tonight."

"Now we can talk about the slumber party, Naomi," Cathy began. "First, what shall we have for dinner?"

They discussed the relative merits of roast turkey and roast beef, avocado salad and orange gelatin salad. Chris suggested her favorite meat loaf and they gave it polite consideration, but discarded this dish as inelegant.

They went on to sleeping arrangements. There were five bedrooms in the Leonard house. On one side of the center hall lay Cathy's and Chris's rooms, joined by a bath. On the other side lay Mother's and Daddy's big room with a bathroom next to it. Then came Jeff's room and the guest room, with a small bath between made from a converted closet.

"Chris," Cathy said, "if you'll sleep with Jeff that night we can have two girls in your room, two in mine, and two in the guest room."

"I don't want to sleep with Jeff," Chris said. "He kicks."

"I knew you'd say that. Oh well, it'll be more fun if we're all together, anyway. Will you sleep in the guest room? We could get some old mattresses or something to put in your room and mine."

Chris saw at once that across the hall she would be completely exiled from the party. "I want to sleep in my own room."

Cathy sighed and exchanged glances with Naomi. "I'll discuss it with Mother. Anyhow, Naomi, I read about a slumber party where they ate pizza pies in the middle of the night. Doesn't that sound super?"

Chris made a small sound of anguish at that, which neither of the girls noticed. She loved pizzas. She made a mental resolution that if they had pizza pies, by hook or by crook she was going to have some too.

At dinner she announced, buttering a warm roll, "I might go to a museum where they have animals during Easter vacation."

"I'm going too," Jeff said promptly.

Chris looked up. This treat was supposed to be for just her and Mother. "You went there," she said. "With Grandma."

"I can go again." Chris opened her mouth to argue, then shut it.

"Mother," she said, as she and Cathy cleared the table, "does Jeff have to go?"

"Why do you object to your brother's going?"

It was hard to explain that Cathy was classing her with Jeff and pushing them both out of her party. "The children," Cathy called them. If Jeff went along, Chris felt she would be accepting this classification. An outing shared with Mother alone conferred special status on her. "I want just you to go," she insisted.

Later she wandered into the library, where Daddy was reading his paper, and sat down with an audible sigh. After a time he looked at her. "Have you got a problem, Chrissy?"

"I can't decide whether to go to a museum, or what, for my special treat. Daddy, can you suggest something else?"

"Your mother might take you to a play."

But the school play seemed to fulfill Chris's yearning for drama. She could think of nothing exciting and special enough to make up for the slumber party. She sat dejectedly as Mother came in with her knitting.

"Chrissy has problems about Easter week," Daddy said.

"We'll think of something," said Mother.

"I may have to go to Detroit that week," Daddy remarked, going back to his newspaper. Daddy was vice-president of a company, and sometimes traveled on business.

The days passed. Now the yard was filled with

glossy starlings and tiny, ruddy fox sparrows, furiously gathering leaves and twigs. Gray squirrels crammed wads of blown paper into their mouths and leaped across the lawn. Buds swelled amidst the daffodil leaves. And the Friday of Cathy's slumber party was almost here.

Cathy had solved the problem of sleeping arrangements to her own satisfaction and Chris's chagrin. Mother said the girls could sleep on the floor in the living room. There was plenty of room for six there and in the adjoining television room. They could bring mattresses from upstairs and borrow others and, with the door into the hall closed, they were quite safe from intrusion. They could even watch the late, late, late or early, early show.

Dinner was to be served the guests in the dining room, and not only Chris and Jeff but Mother and Daddy would eat in the kitchen. Chris gave in with outward grace. Secretly, she plotted.

"I'll clear the table for dessert for you, Cathy," she offered one afternoon, as Cathy and Mother were discussing the dinner.

Cathy raised her eyebrows. "I don't know whether you would do it properly."

"I do it every night," Chris cried.

"Yes, but when you wait on *guests,* you do *not* pile up messy plates."

Chris had an inspiration. "Cathy, why don't I have a white apron and a little white cap and really be a waitress, just like one in a restaurant?"

The idea struck a responsive chord, but Cathy had some doubts. "Do you know about 'place to the right, pass to the left'?"

"What's that?"

"I'll show you." Cathy marched into the dining room and sat down. "I'm a guest. When you pass me something, like rolls, you pass it on my left side. Pass me something."

Chris looked around, saw a bowl of fruit on the sideboard, and passed it to Cathy.

"Why, thank you." Cathy helped herself to the last banana, peeled it down, and took a bite.

"Give me some," the waitress said, watching hungrily.

Cathy giggled and broke off a piece. "Now you have to *place* something in front of me, such as a plate of roast beef and potatoes and stuff. Get something to place."

Chris obediently went into the kitchen for

something to place. As she looked around, her glance fell on the cats' saucer on the floor, half full of cat food that Mr. Pickle scorned now the field-mouse season was on. Chris gave a small giggle, picked up the saucer, and marched into the dining room.

"To the right," Cathy sang. "To the right—oh!" She gazed at the saucer in front of her in astonishment and after a moment both guest and waitress burst into a storm of mirth.

"Oh, Chris, you're so silly!" Cathy finally wiped her eyes. "If you promise not to serve cat food you can wait on table. I'll make you a little cap."

On the day of the slumber party Martha and Gretchen arrived after school with their overnight bags. Naomi and her mother brought Pat from the station, and Mother, Cathy, and her guests departed to meet Judy's bus in Springdale.

Chris hovered in the hall as the assembled guests poured in. "Let's all go up to my room," Cathy told them. "That will be the dressing room, even though we're going to sleep downstairs. Look!" She threw open the door into the living room to display three mattresses laid out on the floor and another in the television room. "One can sleep on the sofa and one on the couch." They exclaimed excitedly over the arrangements. "Come on up now."

Chris watched them troop up the stairs and disappear into Cathy's room. After a while she followed softly and went into her own room. The doors to the bathroom between her room and Cathy's stood ajar.

I have to wash my face and get neat for dinner, she decided, and went into the bathroom. They were making too much noise in Cathy's room to hear her, and Chris took all the time she could, listening in on the gaiety, until Judy suddenly pushed open the door. "Oh, excuse me, Chris."

"I'm going right out," Chris said hastily.

Then it was time for dinner, and Cathy came into Chris's room long enough to pin the small white cap she had made to Chris's flyaway hair and to whisper sternly, "Remember, place to the right!"

There was roast beef for dinner, and they had roasted potatoes and asparagus, and the orange gelatin salad Cathy had decided on, and hot rolls and green tomato pickles and jelly. Daddy carved in the kitchen, and Chris served, taking all the time she could, so she could be in the dining room.

Mother had given Cathy a bell to ring when she wanted the waitress. The rest of the family ate calmly enough in the kitchen, but Chris kept waiting for the bell to summon her into the midst of the party. "Maybe we can't hear it," she suggested.

"We can," Mother assured her.

"I'll just go and see if they need anything." She tiptoed to the door and pushed it open hopefully, but no one summoned her.

When the bell did ring they wanted not dessert, but more of everything else. Chris rushed around taking in the refilled plates. She was doing beautifully, remembering each time to place the plate from the guest's right side.

"Will you kindly pass the orange aspic, Norah or Josephine or whatever your name is?" Cathy instructed the maid.

Chris passed the salad, on its serving dish. But she had been "placing" to the right, and for just a moment she forgot that now she was "passing." She passed the salad to Judy from the right side.

Cathy was sitting next to Judy. "Left!" she hissed at the waitress.

Chris jumped. Her hand jerked back and she swung about abruptly. As she did so, the gelatin mold sailed off the plate, landing squarely in Cathy's lap.

"Whoops!" cried Cathy and Chris in the same breath.

For a startled moment Chris expected the wrath of the gods to descend. After Cathy had coached her so carefully! Then Cathy calmly picked up the salad, Chris automatically held out the plate, and Cathy dumped it back on.

The girls were laughing. "Nothing happened," Cathy announced loftily. "Won't you have some aspic, Miss McArdle?" she inquired graciously of Martha.

"Whoops!" cried Naomi, and they all burst into laughter again.

What a relief! Cathy was having too good a time to be cross at her. Chris hovered, laughing in sympathy with the merriment. "You may go now, Josephine," Cathy finally ordered, and Chris departed reluctantly.

Dessert was ice cream with the makings of sundaes. Chris carried in the dishes of mixed fruit, fudge sauce, nuts, and whipped cream with utmost caution. The girls, she noticed, took all four.

Then the well-fed guests trooped into the living room to play games and listen to records.

"Are you going to help me with the dishes, Chris?" Mother inquired, beginning to scrape and rinse the plates.

Chris gave a small moan and gazed at the mess. "Just a minute. I want to see where Fluff is."

She went in and cautiously opened the living-room door. The girls were sitting on the floor, choosing records. Cathy looked up. "What do you want?"

"I wanted to see if Fluff is here."

"He isn't."

Chris dried the dishes. When the kitchen was finally in order, she went back into the hall, opened the living-room door a crack, and peeked in. Music and merriment gushed forth. Again, Cathy was the one to see her. She got up and came over to the door.

"Hello, Chris. Good night, Chris." Cathy pulled the door shut, gently but firmly.

The girls went upstairs at last to don pajamas and collect blankets. They went down again, though not to sleep. Chris got herself into bed, but she had no intention of going to sleep either. Somehow she was going to get into the kitchen when pizza time came. She left her light on.

But she did go to sleep, and awoke with a start of alarm to darkness and quiet. Mother must have turned her light off. What were the girls doing?

They must be in the kitchen. Oh, she hoped she wasn't too late! Chris got up hastily and went partway downstairs. Yes, the open door showed the living room empty, and from the back of the house came faint sounds. The girls were singing.

Well, she had a right to get a glass of milk. Chris went through the house and paused at the closed kitchen door. They were singing a French round they had all learned in kindergarten. *"Frère Jacques, Frère Jacques, dormez-vous, dormez-vous. . . ."* She opened the door and edged in. They were sitting around the table, and in front of them were not only pizza pies but the remains of the roast beef, pickles, milk, and Coca-Cola bottles. A mouth-watering aroma filled the air.

"Chris, what are you doing here?" Cathy demanded.

"I want to get a glass of milk."

"Well, get it and take it upstairs."

"Do you want a piece of pizza, Chris?" Naomi asked, and handed her a wedge. Chris devoured the tomatoey, cheesey morsel. Delicious! She looked hungrily at the table.

"What's that noise?" Pat asked.

From inside the cellar came a soft whine, then a bark. Rover, who slept in the basement now, had recognized Chris's voice. "That's Chris's dog," Cathy said.

"Shall I let him out?" Chris asked hopefully. Rover might occupy their attention and prolong her stay.

"Yes!" cried Pat and Judy.

"No!" cried Cathy.

But Chris was already opening the door, only to have it knocked out of her hand by the emerging Rover. Panting with joy, sniffing mightily, Rover galloped across the kitchen, plopped his great front paws in Martha's lap, and reached ravenously for the wonderful-smelling food on her plate. Taken by surprise, Martha drew back with a squeal, and her chair went over. Rover gobbled the pizza and passed on to the next plate.

The girls were helpless with laughter. Cathy

and Chris together got hold of the dog and pulled and shoved him back into the cellarway.

"Now good *night,* Chris!" Cathy shouted over the din.

There was still part of a pizza pie, and she simply had to have another piece. "Can't I have. . . ."

"Here." Cathy scooped up the pizza, poured a glass of milk, and put them in Chris's hands. She moved her toward the door. "Good night, my *dear* little sister!"

The mattress beds were neatly made up. Chris glanced in longingly as she started upstairs, but she didn't quite dare ask to sleep down here and try Cathy further.

She sat on her bed, munching and sipping, making the wonderful food last as long as possible. Then Chris licked her fingers, got into bed, and turned out the light. The slumber party was over, so far as she was concerned, but she had had a small part in it, after all.

CHAPTER FOUR

THE KEY WON'T TURN

Chris was on her way to school. It was raining this morning, a gentle patter that drew the strong smell of spring out of the rich earth. Instead of cutting through the soaked fields she sloshed in the puddles by the edge of the road.

It was the Monday after the slumber party. Chris had seen Cathy and Naomi onto the bus, as usual. They were in high spirits, endlessly reviewing the fun.

She herself was feeling listless and bored. She had managed to squeeze into the pizza part of the party, but otherwise there had been no bending of Cathy's intention to exclude her. She had nothing to be particularly happy about this morning.

Besides, she had heard Judy say to Cathy,

"When you come to spend the night during Easter vacation. . . ." This meant Cathy had further plans that did not include her. As for herself, she was still unable to think of a treat that could come near to equaling Cathy's social life.

She turned her head at a soft sound beside her. Rover had appeared from somewhere, pink tongue lolling out, delighted to encounter her.

"Hello, Rover." She stood still to stroke his wet head and gaze into the brown eyes that searched hers adoringly. Here was one friend who loved her, who asked no greater happiness than to be with her. Chris felt her battered spirits being soothed by Rover's love. He trotted beside her, perking up his ears as she talked to him.

Because it was raining, the pupils had gone in early. Chris said good-by to Rover. "You be a good boy now and go home." He stood there, eyes bright, tail moving slightly in camaraderie, as he watched her go into the building.

In Chris's room the pupils were killing time in various ways until the bell rang. Janice and Emily and some of the others in the play were clustered in a corner. From what she could hear, Chris knew they were discussing costumes. The left-out feeling came back. She took out her reading book and pretended to be absorbed. When the bell rang and the pupils had to return to their seats, she breathed a sigh of relief.

It was half an hour later when Rover arrived. Chris's head was bent over her arithmetic paper when she became aware of a commotion in the front of the room, and looked up. The door had been ajar. There was Rover, first greeting Mrs. Franz with cordiality, then eluding her hand and starting briskly down the first aisle to sniff at each child and to swipe one here and there with a moist tongue.

The children were charmed. Laughter arose and they reached out for him. Rover paused to give his wet coat a shake. The boys shouted, and girls dodged the shower of drops, squealing.

"Does this animal belong to any of you?" Mrs. Franz demanded, joining in the mirth.

One of the boys, Larry, raised his hand, but Chris spoke up. "He's mine."

"Well, for goodness' sake, Chris, get him out of here."

But now Rover had discovered her, and he was clambering over her, delirious with joy. She had to push him away to get out of her seat and grasp him by the scruff.

Larry had stood up and was looking at Rover intently. "He looks just like a dog that used to live near me."

"Well, he's mine," Chris repeated firmly.

She escorted him downstairs and out the door. She could hear him scratching and whining with disappointment as she turned away.

Larry spoke to her again as she went back to

her seat. "Hey, Chris, are you sure that's your dog?"

"Of course I am." She refused to consider any other possibility. "His name is Rover."

"That's sure funny." Larry shook his head.

She thought of Larry's query once or twice during the morning, but put it out of her mind.

At noon Mother said, "I'm going to pick Cathy up after school and take her to the dentist."

"I'm going to Mike's," Jeff announced.

"I'll stay for rehearsal," Chris said.

"Well, I'll leave the back door unlocked," Mother told her. "Mrs. Hughes will be home, in case you want her."

Chris opened the back door that afternoon feeling quite grown up. She was practically never alone in the house. For some reason, she tiptoed as she took off her sweater and laid down her books. Even empty, the house seemed alive, with small voices of its own—the purr of the refrigerator, the settling of a pipe, the brief rumble of the electric water pump.

She opened the refrigerator and got out milk, and spread a piece of bread lavishly with peanut butter. Eating, she strolled through the rooms in luxurious solitude, stopping to talk to the parakeet. Fluff uncurled from a chair in the library with a small "prrp" of welcome, and she tucked him under her chin.

Then Chris carefully washed her glass and plate and knife, and put them away. It gave her a feeling of special responsibility to be in charge of the house, and she wiped off the sink. She gave Fluff a final squeeze, filled Rover's dish, and went out the back door to call him. The rain had stopped, and the sun had come out on a world of green and growing things.

He came galloping out of the orchard, and Chris watched with her usual satisfaction as he wolfed down his meal. "What were you thinking of to come into school!" she demanded sternly.

With the dog at her heels, Chris set out at a trot for the orchard, picking up a stick to throw as she ran.

They were having their usual gay romp when Rover paused suddenly, ears erect, and looked back at the house. Chris followed his gaze. A car had turned into the driveway, and seemed to be stopping at the front door. Suddenly Rover made a strange sound in his throat, and took off.

"Rover!" Chris cried, and followed. Then she heard the driver of the car whistle.

Rover reached the man, who had stepped out of the car, and was leaping and barking like a dog gone mad.

"Take it easy, Prince, old boy, take it easy!" the man was saying as Chris finally caught up. He looked up. "Hello, there. This is my dog! We thought we'd lost him forever."

Chris was totally unprepared for the blow. She stopped as if she had been struck speechless.

"A youngster who lives near us told us he thought he saw him," the man said. "How long has he been here?"

Her tongue loosened. "We caught him in a trap. Not a hurting trap. Because he barked and kept my mother and father awake. But I didn't want the state trooper to take him away, so now I feed him, and he sleeps in our basement."

"Well, I think he'll be glad to get home." The man fondled the dog's head. "I live about two miles from here, and I don't know how he happened to wander so far. Want to go home, Prince?" he asked.

Prince barked enthusiastically.

"But . . . but . . . he likes it here! I. . . ." Chris knelt suddenly, put her arms around Rover's neck, and buried her face in his coat.

After a moment the man spoke gently. "I'm sorry to take him away. But my kids love him, too, you know. We'd better get going." Chris drew herself away from the dog. "Come on, Prince, in the car. Thanks very much for looking after him. I really appreciate it." He held out his hand, and Chris put hers in it.

She watched as the engine spurted into action, and the car began to move down the drive. From the rear she could see the two figures, the driver and the dog sitting importantly beside him. Already Rover had forgotten her, his friend. Then the car turned into the road, the man waved, and they vanished.

Chris began to weep. Larry was the one. He had told the man! Crying bitterly, stricken at her loss, she started blindly around to the back door. As she went in, she heard Naomi's door open, and Mrs. Hughes called, "Chris, are you all right?" Chris went on without answering, moaning and talking to herself to fill up the vast emptiness that suddenly surrounded her.

"I haven't even got a dog friend now," Chris was sobbing to herself. "I haven't got anybody. I haven't even got—plans!" Blindly she hunted about for Fluff, but he was nowhere to be found. Crying harder and harder, she stumbled up the stairs to her room and threw herself on the bed, surrendering to the sobs that shook her whole body.

Not only the loss of Rover, but all the remembered hurt at Cathy's not wanting her to share in the slumber party, at being left out of the school play, at Janice's desertion, poured out with the sobs. Chris lay there and cried until she was exhausted.

She checked herself suddenly and raised her head. "Chris!" That was Naomi's voice downstairs. Chris got hastily to her feet and closed her bedroom door softly. She didn't want anyone to see her crying so hard. "Are you all right, Chrissy?" Naomi called.

"Yes," Chris said through the door.

"Isn't Cathy home yet?"

"No."

Naomi departed, and the tears began again. She didn't want Naomi there, but she felt desolate all by herself. Cathy and Naomi, always together. A blank, blank future stretched endlessly ahead. Finally, almost alarmed by the racking sobs she could not stop, and seeking some sort of comfort, Chris opened her door and wandered down the hall into her mother's room. She felt a little soothed by the familiar slight fragrance that always hung about this room. The sobs became smaller. Chris went into Mother's bathroom to get a drink.

Letting the water run, she caught a glimpse of herself in the mirror. How awful she looked. Eyes all red, nose red, hair mussed. Then she heard a car door slam in the back of the house. The family was home. With a sudden instinctive desire to hide herself and her trouble, Chris hastily locked the bathroom door.

They were calling. "Chris, are you up there?" That was Cathy. She did not answer.

Jeff came upstairs. "Chris, where are you?" He was going into her room. Finally he arrived at the bathroom door in his mother's room. "Are you in there, Chris?" He tried the door. Still she was silent.

Jeff went down and Cathy ran upstairs. "Chris,

are you in the bathroom? What's the matter? Why don't you open the door!" She rattled the knob.

"I don't want to."

Then Mother was there. "Chris, open the door."

She had to face them. Sniffing and giving a swipe at her nose with the back of her hand, Chris took hold of the key. She could not turn it.

"What is the matter, Chris? Open this door."

"I can't." She struggled with the key, but it would not turn.

"Take the key out of the lock and push it under the door," Mother instructed.

She couldn't. The key would neither turn nor allow itself to be removed.

"Well, I don't know why you locked it," Mother said, "but now you'll have to wait until Daddy comes home and can put up the ladder."

Chris began to cry again, helplessly. "How soon will he get here?"

"In about an hour."

"Cathy bought some candy, Chris," Jeff announced, outside the door.

"Don't tell her that!" Cathy exclaimed. "You'll just make her hungry."

"Chris," Mother said, "are you crying?"

"Y-es."

"Because you're locked in? Or did something happen?"

"Some-thing ha-happened."

"What?"

"Ro-over went—away. A man—came—for him."

"Oh!" Chris heard Cathy exclaim softly, in sympathy.

Then Mother said, "Well, dear, be glad he has found his own home. Suppose you lost Fluff. Wouldn't you be happy if someone found him and brought him home?"

"I—wanted—him—to stay!"

"Oh, poor Chris, all alone!" Cathy cried.

It was difficult for Mother to comfort her with a locked door between them. "Anyhow, honey, just be patient," she said, "and Daddy will be home very soon now. He'll get you out. Maybe you can curl up there and take a little nap."

"I'm—not—sleepy."

"Chris, don't cry, and I'll sit out here and play a game with you," Cathy offered.

"I don't w-want to."

"Oh yes, it's fun. You name something blue

you can see from where you are, and I'll name something blue I can see from where I am, and we'll see who can find the most blue things. Don't you want to?"

Behind the locked door Chris gave another sob and nodded gravely.

"Don't you want to, Chris?" Cathy insisted.

"Yes." She was still shaken by weeping, but it helped to have Cathy there.

When they exhausted the blues they went on to the pinks, and suddenly Chris found herself laughing in spite of herself. "Chris, do you know what you could do?" Cathy said, when pinks were used up too. "You could take a bath. Think of the gorgeous long bath you could have had if you'd just started sooner."

"What does she want to take a bath for?" Jeff shouted, stamping upstairs to check on the situation. Chris was inclined to agree. Cathy invented another game, and left Jeff to play it while she went down to set the table. Chris felt much calmer now.

Daddy finally came home. Jeff went scrambling downstairs, shouting the news of Chris's imprisonment, and then came what seemed the longest

wait of all, while Daddy changed into slacks and
got the ladder. Chris heard its thud against the
house and ran to the window. At last Daddy's
head appeared. She pushed the window up, and
he climbed in.

"Well, imagine meeting you here!" said Daddy,
giving her tear-stained face a kiss.

He had to work with the key, bracing his knee
against the door and pushing and pulling the
knob. But suddenly something gave, the key
turned, the lock clicked, and the door was open.
Mother, Cathy, and Jeff all stood anxiously waiting.

"Welcome home!" said Mother, gathering
Chris into her arms.

Cathy laughed joyously, and Jeff jumped up
and down until Daddy said, "You'll knock down
the plaster."

"Dinner's ready, come on," Mother said, Chris
still clinging to her hand.

"I'll have to wash my hands and face," said
Chris.

"What! In the bathroom two hours, and now
you have to go back and wash your face?" said
Daddy. "Don't lock the door, please."

Chris descended to dinner at last, only a suspicion of pinkness about her shiny face, and her locks combed into place. She had an odd combination of feelings as she slid into her chair at the table and faced the family. Partly she felt guilty at having locked herself in and caused so much trouble. Partly she felt like a heroine. She still felt desolate over Rover, too. She ate her dinner soberly, not joining much in the conversation or responding to Mother's and Cathy's efforts to be gay and cheer her up.

She thought of still another grievance. "Cathy," she said plaintively, "are you going to Judy's house, Easter vacation?"

Cathy looked quickly at Mother, and there was a moment's silence. It was then that Daddy, passing a second helping to Jeff, his spoon in the chicken casserole, said, "Which day does your your birthday come on, Chris?"

"Wednesday after Easter."

Daddy glanced across at Mother, and Chris saw Mother nod. Daddy began to serve Cathy. "That would fit in all right with a plan I was going to mention."

"What?" Cathy asked.

"What?" said Jeff.

"What plan?" Chris echoed.

"It's a plan for Chris." Daddy handed Cathy her plate. "You've been trying to think of something special to do Easter week, haven't you, Chris?"

She nodded.

"I have to make a quick business trip to Detroit," Daddy said. "How would you like to go with me?"

CHAPTER FIVE
CHRIS MAKES PLANS

A bomb could have evoked no greater explosion than Daddy's matter-of-fact question. Cathy and Chris both gasped. Jeff shouted, "Oh, boy, go to Detroit! Where's that?" Mother laughed at all of them.

Then Chris collected herself. "Oh, yes, yes," she cried. "I do want to! Are we going in the car?"

"On the train."

Jeff suddenly slid out of his chair and went around to his father. "I can't go too, can I?"

"Not this time, Son." Daddy put an arm around him. Jeff lay down on the floor on his stomach, in a favorite posture of revolt that he had almost outgrown, but in a moment he thought better of it and got up. This was too interesting to interrupt with tantrums.

"We'll be on the train overnight on Monday," Daddy was explaining to Chris. "We'll be in Detroit Tuesday, and then we'll fly home on Wednesday."

Chris heard Cathy give another gasp. "Fly?" Chris asked. "In an airplane?"

"Did you think on wings?" Cathy said. "You're no angel, Chris."

Chris jumped up and fluttered about the room, waving her arms. "I'm flying home, I'm flying home!" she crooned. All unhappy episodes of the recent past had magically faded from her mind, and in their place unfolded glorious vistas of adventure.

She could not eat much dinner after that. Then there were dishes to be washed, in spite of all the excitement. "Boy, you're lucky, Chris!" Cathy said, as she washed the dishes and Chris dried them.

"Your turn will come," Chris told her, a trifle smugly.

"Oh, don't worry about me," Cathy retorted loftily. "I couldn't go, anyway. I'm going to Judy's for another slumber party."

Chris scarcely heard her. "Mother, what suitcase shall I take?"

Mother was involved in persuading Jeff that a pending trip for Chris was no reason for delaying his bedtime, so Chris slipped out of the kitchen. She remembered seeing a suitcase in the linen closet, and she went up and dragged it out. She came downstairs with the enormous bag thumping on each step. "Shall I take this one?" she asked.

"Oh, Chris!" Mother said, laughing. "That's five times as big as you need. You may take my train case. But don't worry about your luggage yet. You're not going for ten days."

Next morning Chris was awake early, filled with eager anticipation of exciting things to come. She was dressed when Cathy came in.

"I was going to go down and take a run with Rover, and then I remembered he wasn't here any more," Chris said with a little laugh. The tragedy of yesterday seemed a long time back and not really too important now.

At breakfast she was full of questions, a delayed reaction to last night. "What shall I wear when I go?" she wanted to know.

"A sweater or blouse and skirt," Mother told her. "You can take a dress with you."

Chris nodded. "A sweater would be good, be-

cause it hasn't got any buttons. What coat shall I wear?"

"You're due for a new spring coat. We'll get it before Easter."

"Do I have to wear a hat?"

"Oh, I think so," said Mother.

"Of course you have to wear a hat on a train overnight, Chris," Cathy put in.

"Overnight? Does she have to wear it overnight?" Jeff demanded in astonishment.

They all laughed, and Cathy said, "Jeff, you are a silly billy boy."

Chris looked at her rebukingly, defending Jeff. "You don't know everything, Cathy. You never went on a train overnight."

"No, but I've got some sense." Cathy gave a sniff.

Chris turned back to her mother. She was quite aware that her sister was as interested as she in learning the correct attire for a young lady taking a train to Detroit, but if Cathy wanted to act superior it was perfectly all right with her.

She was eager to get to school and announce to everyone that she was going to Detroit. This morning it didn't matter that Janice and Emily would be huddled together somewhere. Fortified by her momentous news, she would walk right in on them.

"I think I'll take my lunch," she announced.

Mother looked astonished. Even on snowy days Chris preferred to come home. "Well, fine," she said. "I'll make you some sandwiches. Get yourself a banana and some cookies."

Usually she loitered, going to school. Today Chris was brisk. On the playground she advanced directly on Janice and Emily. "Know what?" she cried.

They did not know what. Chris told them. "My father is going to Detroit on business during Easter vacation, and I'm going with him! On the train!"

They looked suitably impressed. They regarded her respectfully. "Is that far?" Emily asked.

"Yes! We're going to sleep on the train. And we're going to fly home in an airplane!"

This was big-time news, and games and conversation were suspended by all within hearing to give due consideration to Chris's coming adventure. One by one the other girls in the class gathered to find out what the excitement was about.

No one in this group had ever slept on a train, and only one girl had traveled by air. Chris was the center of it all, happy, excited. Quite carried away by this unprecedented attention, she found herself chattering on, embellishing the tale by adding bits about Mother's train case and dinner in the diner.

When they went into school she wasted no time before telling Mrs. Franz. The teacher showed them where Detroit was on the map, and told them that automobiles were made there. She also pointed out that Detroit was close to Canada, which was a foreign country.

By now Chris had become a very important person in the fourth grade, and at recess several girls requested the honor of playing hopscotch with her. At noon she ate her lunch with Janice and Emily.

It was then that Janice put aside their past difference and made a gesture of friendship. "Chris, I just thought of something. I've got a pretty little zipper case—all pink, with roses. It's called a toilet case. It's to put your soap and washcloth and toothbrush in. You can borrow it to take to Detroit, if you want to."

Chris felt quite overcome.

Emily was not to be outdone, and spoke up quickly. "You can borrow my new umbrella if you want to, too."

This seemed a sound idea, for who could know what the weather might be in a far-distant place like Detroit?

Then Janice came up with another and truly radical suggestion. "Chris, why don't you come to my house after school? You can see if you like the little zipper case."

Never had Chris gone home with another girl after school. It took her a while to adjust to the idea. "I'll have to ask my mother if she'll take me."

"You can go on the bus with me," Janice cried.

"Call your mother from the office and ask her," Emily suggested. "Call her now before the bell rings."

Flustered, but supported by Janice and Emily ˙n person, Chris hurried to the principal's office. Miss Metz, please may I telephone my mother?"

Miss Metz looked at them. "Is anything wrong?"

"No. I just want to tell her I'm going home with Janice on the school bus."

Mother sounded alarmed, too, when she heard

Chris's voice. "Chris! What's the matter?" She was relieved and very much surprised when Chris told her the plan.

When she hung up, Chris felt impelled to tell Miss Metz about her trip, and why the expedition to Janice's house was so important. The principal agreed that these were matters of moment.

It was Chris's first ride on the school bus, and she found herself caught up in the noisy, chattering crowd. In no time she was screaming like all the others to make herself heard.

Emily got off the bus some time before they reached Janice's house. She could not come to play today, but she promised to bring the umbrella to school. Chris was rather glad when Emily left them. She was a nice girl, but Janice was the one who had proffered friendship. Chris was glad to be back on the right track with Janice.

Janice's mother gave them cookies and milk. Chris approved the pretty, pink-flowered case, and laid it carefully with her books to take home. Then they spent a companionable hour, chattering and swinging in Janice's rope swing. Chris had never been happier.

Mother came to get her at five. As she climbed

into the car, Janice called, "Don't forget to bring your lunch tomorrow. You can help Emily and me learn our parts." Chris rode home in a rosy glow. Janice wasn't mad at her any more, and they were friends.

At dinner she bubbled about her afternoon. Having a new friend had actually edged out, just for the moment, excitement over the trip. But she had many unanswered questions for Daddy, some of which had been asked her at school, and she calmed down and came around to them before dinner was over.

"What will I do in Detroit, Daddy?"

"This man I have to see, Rod Hammersmith, has a family," Daddy told her. "I'm not sure, but I think he has children about your age. I'm going to see if we can fix you up for the day."

In spite of the assurance engendered by her new prominence in school, Chris felt a sudden stab of doubt. She had pictured herself spending the day in Detroit with Daddy, not with strangers.

"Won't that be fun, Chris?" Mother said, as if reading her thoughts.

"But I don't know if I'll like. . . ." Chris began. "I mean, it would be different if Cathy and Jeff were there and. . . ."

"Oh, come on, Chris," Daddy said good-naturedly, "you can't be sandwiched in between your brother and sister for the rest of your life."

"You'll be on your own, Chris," Cathy told her heartlessly. "You can't be a clinging vine in Detroit." She gave a chuckle. "This is like launching a ship. Chris is being launched—on the sea of life!" she proclaimed dramatically.

They all laughed, even Chris, and Cathy cried, "We ought to break a bottle of ginger ale on your head, the way they do with boats, Chris!"

Jeff reached over to pretend he was breaking a bottle, and Chris protected her head, giggling, and forgot her doubts.

It was then that Cathy, seizing a lighthearted moment, said with studied casualness, eyes on her plate, "By the way, Chris, I'm going to Judy's the Wednesday after Easter."

Chris looked up. "That's the day I come home. And that's my birthday."

"So?" Cathy said.

"Don't be rude, Cathy," said Mother.

"Then you won't be here for my birthday dinner!" Chris cried. "Everybody in the family is always home for birthday dinners!"

"I know, Chrissy." Cathy looked up at last, her face serious. "But what can I do? I said I could go any day. I didn't know you were going to Detroit, and I never thought about your birthday. And Judy's invited some other kids. I'll give you something specially nice for your birthday, Chris, to make up," she added.

Chris sat silent.

"I can't spoil Judy's plans!" Cathy cried. "And I can't be two places at once. Anyhow, you'll just be getting home and everything, and you won't even know it's your birthday, you'll be so excited."

"Yes, I will."

"Oh, Chris, you're impossible!" Cathy cried. "You always act hurt, and it's *frustrating!*"

"Now see here, you two," Daddy said, and both girls threw off their tension and relaxed at his tone. "We'll have no more of this. Cathy has all sorts of parties, and Chris is going on a trip. What does it take to satisfy you?"

Suddenly everyone jumped as Jeff's fist came down on the table with a bang, jarring the dishes. "I want to do something special, too!" Jeff roared in a tone of outrage.

For a moment they were all too surprised to speak. Then Daddy said, "Son, you are absolutely right!"

They all burst into laughter at the righteous indignation of their youngest member.

CHAPTER SIX
EASTER

The problem now was what special treat to provide for Jeff. The solution was simple, however. Jeff intended to go and see the dinosaurs again. "And I might go to the zoo, also," he informed his family. They all agreed this expedition could best take place on the day when Chris was in Detroit.

Chris was crossing off on the calendar each day that passed, each day that slowly brought her closer to the great event in her life. The P.T.A. play was drawing closer, too. Chris took her lunch to school every day, and at noon she helped Janice and Emily learn their parts. She was friends with both now, especially Janice.

She had not found a hammock. She was still

counting on Cathy, and Cathy was busy with her own concerns.

One afternoon Chris arrived home just as Cathy got off the bus. "Where's Naomi?" Chris asked.

"She went shopping."

This was an opportunity. Mrs. Franz had inquired about the hammock at rehearsal, and time was growing short. "Cathy," Chris said, "please, will you go out with me and try and find a hammock?"

She scarcely hoped her sister would agree, so it was a delightful surprise when Cathy replied cheerfully, "O.K. I think I remember seeing one in a yard last summer."

They got their bicycles. It was a lovely afternoon. Down by the river they paused to hunt for the long-stemmed blue violets that grew there in the grass. It was too early for violets, but they lingered to listen to the unseen peeper chorus, jingling its silver bells along the stream.

Once across the bridge they were in the country, well-tailored pasturelands bordering the road in both directions, comfortable white farmhouses set far apart. Chris chattered excitedly, as they rode along, about the play and Detroit. It was wonderful to have Cathy to talk to, and she had perfect confidence that her sister would find a hammock.

Cathy did not disappoint her. "The house that had the hammock was right along here. There, that's the one. Let's go in. You ask if they've got a hammock and if you can borrow it."

Chris quailed. "Cathy, you ask."

"I will not!"

"But I don't know the people."

"Neither do I." Then Cathy took pity on her. "Oh, all right, come on."

Memory had served Cathy right. There was a hammock here, and the woman was most gracious about lending it for the play. Her husband would even transport the hammock and stand to school.

Chris was very happy as they pedaled home, mission accomplished. They coasted along, side by side, talking and laughing, the air in their faces. Chris's cheeks felt pink, her hair blown.

"Thank you very much, Cathy," she said, as they put their bicycles away.

"Oh, you're welcome. Too bad you can't be in the play."

"I don't mind," Chris said humbly. She knew it was her own fault.

"Chris. . . ." Cathy was about to say something, then seemed to think better of it. "Never mind."

But solving her sister's problem seemed to have put Cathy in high spirits. Chris, playing a card game with Jeff, looked up in surprise as Cathy began to set the dinner table, then dropped knives and forks with a clatter to come in and sit down at the piano. "Oh, I went down South, for to see my Sal. Sing Polly-wolly-doodle all the day!" she sang lustily.

She spun around, leaped up, and poked her finger into the parakeet's cage. Then she seized Fluff as he meandered through the room, tossed him into the air, and snuggled him under her chin.

"You must feel good, Cathy!" Chris exclaimed with a giggle.

"I do, I do, because I am so good to you!" Cathy caroled in rhyme. "And I just decided something, too."

"What?"

"I won't tell you. Wild horses wouldn't drag it out of me. I have to make a phone call, but I'll be down in a minute."

She came back shortly, humming, to lay the

silver. Chris got out plates and Jeff went clumping around with the napkins. Cathy had them all laughing uproariously at nothing.

One day they all went to Springdale to do their Easter shopping. At Bauman's Department Store Chris chose a black-and-white-checked reefer, and Cathy picked out a navy-blue coat. Chris chose a red straw hat with white flowers at the back, Cathy a white hat. The new Easter dresses were of soft cotton, Chris's yellow, Cathy's blue.

Cathy had new white gloves. Chris was delighted with brown kid ones, on account, Mother explained, of white gloves getting so dirty on the train. This was Chris's first pair of kid gloves, and she not only admired their supple softness, she also sniffed them ecstatically before she allowed the saleswoman to put them in a box. The aroma of the fresh leather was strong and delicious and made her mouth water, and she hoped privately that she could keep from putting these elegant but juicy-smelling new gloves in her mouth and chewing them.

Jeff was impatient with the shopping expedition. He kept wandering off on inspections of his own and returning to complain bitterly about the time they were taking. At last Mother said, "The boys' department is in the basement. Let's go and get Jeff an Easter outfit."

He clumped downstairs willingly enough, but when the salesman brought out a suit in his size Jeff suddenly turned shy.

"Just try on the jacket," Mother urged.

He shook his head. Then he sauntered with devious purpose away from the family group.

"Jeff, come back here, please," Mother called.

"I'll get him." Cathy marched after her small brother.

Two short opposite flights of stairs met at a landing and went on up to Bauman's main floor. Jeff rounded the bottom of the farther flight, and eyed Cathy.

"Come here, Jeffy, I want to tell you a secret."

He was not to be trapped by that old trick. Jeff slowly mounted the stairs, eyes on Cathy. Cathy started up the nearer flight, and he promptly descended on his side, and hovered.

Chris came to Cathy's assistance. As he saw his sisters about to close in, Jeff ran nimbly up the stairs and disappeared.

They all went up. Chris caught a glimpse of Jeff hovering in the rear of the store. She went toward him, and Jeff, eyeing her approach, began backing away. He backed into a rack of clothes. But the rack was on rollers, and Jeff suddenly lost his balance, took three or four back, running steps, and sat down hard on the floor as the rack of clothes sailed off.

His dignity was damaged. Jeff refused to be assisted and sat there. "Just ignore him, then," Mother finally instructed, and out they went to the car, Cathy and Chris trying their best to keep giggles under control. Jeff had looked so funny and surprised when he sat down!

"I'll bet it hurt!" Chris said, and they laughed heartlessly at Jeff's discomfiture.

After a while Jeff wordlessly opened the rear door of the car and climbed in by himself.

"I guess some boys just don't appreciate new clothes," Mother remarked, as she started the engine.

Silence in the back seat. Chris decided to try her influence. "I certainly appreciate my new clothes," she announced loudly over her shoulder. "I certainly do appreciate my new clothes!" But Jeff showed no evidence of being impressed by this obvious performance.

Cathy and Chris both ran upstairs when they got home, to try on their Easter finery. Coming down, complete with hat, coat, and gloves, Chris heard Jeff finally exchanging words with his mother. "May I please speak to you?" he was saying politely.

"Go right ahead," said Mother.

"I mean in the library."

When they emerged, hand in hand, Jeff was looking vastly relieved. "There were too many women around to try on clothes," Mother explained.

So there had to be a second trip to Springdale. Cathy and Chris went along, but not to help Jeff select a suit. "Chris," Cathy said as they started, "by the way, is there anything special you had in mind for your birthday?"

"Yes," Chris replied promptly. "I'd like one of those dolls with hair you can wash, and I'd like some jewelry, and, oh yes, a book about birds—I mean how to tell what bird it is. And a box to put handkerchiefs in. Oh, and some handkerchiefs, real pretty grown-up ones. And some dungarees and shirts and socks and. . . . Well, that'll give you some ideas."

"Whatever gave you the notion I was looking for two thousand ideas?" Cathy demanded.

"You said you were going to give me something specially nice."

"That's right, I did," Cathy said. "You're like an elephant, Chris, you never forget."

Chris paid a visit to the five-and-ten in Springdale; Cathy went off on her own; and Mother and Jeff departed for Bauman's lower regions. When Chris met the rest of the family later, Jeff was carrying a suit box and wearing a beatific expression. And examining Cathy closely, Chris saw something lumpy that her sister was clutching under her jacket.

The P.T.A. play was a huge success. The Leonards all attended. Having done her part in the preparations, Chris sat in the audience between Cathy and Jeff. Even though the trip to Detroit had overshadowed the play, now that the night had come there was envy in her soul of the actors and actresses. Their cheeks were red with rouge, their eyes bright with excitement and importance. Being in a play was fun, and she had missed out. She made a resolution that she would never make that mistake again.

"Well, Chris," Cathy said, when the play was over, "it was very good, and I think getting the hammock and things was just as important as being in it."

So Cathy must know she had secretly wanted very much to be in the play, Chris thought to herself. Cathy was trying to make her feel better.

Then it was Easter Sunday. The day was warm enough for them to wear the spring coats, although Chris had not had the slightest intention of not wearing hers, even if it snowed.

She was downstairs with Cathy and Jeff long

before breakfast, to hunt for the Easter eggs that she and Cathy had hidden after Jeff was in bed. There were pink baskets and purple baskets filled with bright green artificial grass, in which nestled jelly beans and little yellow marshmallow chickens; there were chocolate eggs in silver paper, and plain eggs, dyed lavender and blue, hidden behind doors and chairs.

They had scrambled eggs for breakfast, and fresh coffee cake studded with pecans. The sun streaming over the table had a special luminescence this morning, and the sweetness of potted pink hyacinths hung strongly on the air.

At the eleven o'clock service the church was hushed, filled with the pointing flames of white candles and the fragrance of lilies. Chris listened raptly to the story of the Easter rebirth. Even Jeff, beside her, seemed caught up in the immortal wonder.

Easter dinner was at midday. They had pink-fleshed spring lamb, with mint sauce, and peas and new potatoes. And after dinner the great moment arrived when Chris could at long last begin to pack her suitcase. She had been waiting for this moment forever, it seemed to her. Now she brought

Mother's blue train case downstairs and proceeded
to carry down the articles that she had laid out on
her bed.

"Honey," Mother protested, "why don't you do
that upstairs?"

"I'd rather do it where everybody is."

Cathy finally groaned at Chris's up-and-down
trips. "I'm going out to Naomi's."

Chris sat back on her heels beside the suitcase.
"Cathy, are you coming to the station tomorrow to
see me off?"

"I can't."

"Why not?"

"I'm going to the movies with Naomi and
Martha and Gretchen."

"Oh." She didn't really mind too much her
sister's not coming to see her off. What did hurt
was that Cathy would not be at the airport when
she got importantly off the plane, or home for her
birthday dinner. She would be at Judy's. Chris
gave a small regretful sigh.

"You're going to have a super time, Chris,"
Cathy said lightly.

A little later Chris happened to glance out, and
saw Cathy and Naomi, still in their Easter finery,

walking along the road to Martha's house. Suddenly she was tired of packing. Anyhow, she had packed and repacked everything she could think of. She closed the case and followed the girls. They were all sitting on the porch steps.

"Chris," Cathy said severely, "why in the world did you come out in your dungarees and that old shirt on Easter?"

"I had to take off my Easter dress and pack it," Chris explained. "And I don't want to get my good shoes all muddy."

They laughed good-naturedly. "Aren't you taking your dungarees to Detroit?" Naomi asked.

Chris shook her head seriously. "No, I was going to, but. . . . You're teasing me!" she cried.

"Oh, you're cute, Chris," Martha said.

Naomi suddenly hugged herself. "I'm cold, let's go home. Come on, Chrissy." She held out her hand, and Chris took it, reaching out to Cathy with the other. Swinging hands, the three headed home.

Naomi left them at the door. "Chris," Cathy said as they went in, "let's ask Mother if we can get supper. We'll fix something you like, because tomorrow night you'll be away—having an elegant dinner on the train, you lucky girl!"

Chris laughed joyously. "Let's make popovers."

Cathy got out fresh aprons and tied one on Chris. "Why do I have to waste a clean apron when I've got on dirty clothes?" Chris protested.

"I don't know, but you have to," Cathy retorted. "Actually Mother will probably make you change those filthy clothes."

Mother came into the kitchen to give assistance if needed. Cathy got out the cookbook and found the popover recipe, and with some slight advice mixed the batter. Chris cut an onion for potato salad, eyes screwed up against the sting and tears rolling down her cheeks. She set the table before running upstairs to slip into a dress.

They had cold lamb and salad, oversized pop-overs, and cocoa served with marshmallows. It was a gay, candle-lit supper.

"I won't be here tomorrow night," Chris crooned. "I won't be here Tuesday night. Where will we have dinner Tuesday, Daddy?"

"Probably in the hotel."

Chris clapped her hands softly. "But Wednesday night I'll be home, and that's my birthday." Cathy glanced up, and down at her plate again. "You said I'd forget it was my birthday, Cathy, but I won't," Chris informed her.

"I said you were like an elephant."

"We'll have a lovely birthday dinner," Mother said quickly, "and you'll tell Jeff and me all about Detroit. What would you like for your birthday dinner, by the way?"

"My favorite meat loaf, and mashed potatoes, and olives. And butter-pecan ice cream and caramel cake," Chris ordered promptly.

"That's my favorite dinner," Cathy remarked.

"You won't be here," Chris reminded her, this time with satisfaction. "What time will we get home, Daddy?"

"We get into Newark some time after lunch."

"I'll be there to meet you," Jeff informed her.

Mother inquired, "Chris, is there anything Daddy should tell you before he leaves in the morning?"

She had questioned her father many times, but she was only too happy to rehearse instructions again. "Mother is going to put me on the train at the Junction."

"I'll be there, too," said Jeff.

"Your mother will put you in the conductor's charge," Daddy said. "You'll get into Penn Station at five fifteen, and I'll be right on the platform to meet you. That will give us plenty of time to get over to Grand Central. We're taking the Wolverine at six-thirty."

"Wolverine? That's a wild animal, Chris," Cathy cried, and she gave a loud howl, impersonating a wolverine.

Chris felt uncertain at the idea of close association with anything that howled like that, and glanced at her father. "Pay no attention to her," Daddy said, amused. "It's just a train, Chris, a very good train. And it won't bite you."

CHAPTER SEVEN
CHRIS HAS
SOMETHING TO TELL

Chris opened her eyes much earlier than usual, as the long-awaited day dawned at last. She turned her head to look at the windows, and saw that sunshine was spilling in around the edges of the shades. It was a happy omen.

She lay thinking about the trip ahead of her this very day. Tomorrow she would wake up on the train. That in itself seemed impossible. The next morning she would open her eyes in the unknown city of Detroit. And the day after that, she would be right here again, safe in her own bed. It seemed to Chris that by that time she would have changed greatly—how, she could not picture. When she heard Mother go downstairs she pushed off the blanket and got up.

She could not eat breakfast. "Too excited," Mother said, patting her shoulder.

Daddy left for his office with last-minute admonitions. "When you get off the train, start walking toward the gate. I'll meet you."

Chris's heart was beating fast as she stood at the window and watched him board his bus. "Daddy's gone, so the trip has kind of started," she reported, turning away.

Jeff came down, yawning and tousled, while Chris was clearing the table, and she brought him his cereal and fruit juice and talked for a while. When he had eaten, she wandered outdoors into the April morning. Here and there on the wide lawn great golden bursts of forsythia dazzled the eyes, and the magnolia trees were in bloom. More daffodils were out along the side of the house, a row of slender dancers in ruffled skirts, and Chris picked a bunch, breathing their delicate fragrance. Pink and white hyacinths stood stiffly at attention. And although the apple tree was holding its buds tightly furled, under the tree the ground was showing its carpet of violets.

Cathy appeared, still in pajamas, as she went back into the house. Mother was collecting the laundry. "Can I get dressed?" Chris asked. "In my going-away clothes, I mean."

"Certainly not," said Mother. "You've got a whole day ahead of you. Help Cathy with the dishes, and go out and play with Jeff."

"But I don't want to get dirty."

"You can take a bath, I hope, Chris," Cathy called out.

Jeff finally went off to find Mike, Cathy got busy with telephone calls concerning her social engagements, and Chris, after drying the dishes, wandered out to the orchard. The kitchen clock said eight-thirty. It seemed to her as if it ought to be lunchtime, at least.

She was glad to help hang the clothes. She liked to hang clothes. The air smelled sweet, the muddy ground breathed out an earthy pungency, and she stood on tiptoe to reach the line, the sun's warmth on her hair sending her spirits soaring.

"Oh, I just adore clothes on the line!" she cried, when the lines were full, watching the sheets and garments lift and fall and billow in the lazy, soaring dance of the clothesline.

They took their lunch out on the side porch for the first time this spring. "This is the longest day," Chris complained as they ate.

"It certainly is," Cathy agreed. "We're going to the movies at four o'clock, and I simply can't wait. This movie is supposed to be terrific."

"I'm going to the movies, too, some day this week," Jeff announced. "Mike's mother is going to take him and me."

"Naomi's coming to spend the night tonight," Cathy added.

Chris had been dreaming about the train trip, but suddenly these plans that the others were making caught her attention. She looked at Cathy and Jeff, who were going to be here having fun, and for a moment she felt an overpowering impulse to call Daddy and say she wasn't going.

Maybe if she stayed home she could go to the movies too. Maybe she could go to New York with Mother and Jeff. She would love to be here when Naomi spent the night. Suddenly Detroit seemed a hostile place, full of frightening strangers. Home was safe and secure and, as she gazed across the green lawn, the most beautiful place in the world. Why on earth was she thinking of leaving it?

As usual, Cathy seemed to read her mind. "I guess you can't wait to get on that Wolverine, Chris."

So again the home interest dimmed, Detroit loomed. Chris stirred and sighed happily.

She laid out on her bed all the clothes she was planning to wear. Her bag stood packed. Then, for something to do, Chris put her room in order. She straightened things on her bureau and cleared a clutter of books from her desk. Odd pieces of clothing she hung neatly in the closet.

Cathy came in as she finished, and stopped short. "What are you doing, for goodness' sake?"

"Straightening up my room. Doesn't it look nice?"

Cathy looked around, an odd expression on her face. "No."

"It does so!" Chris cried.

"It looks neat, but it doesn't look nice. It looks as if you were dead or something. Why didn't you leave it messy and natural?"

Chris looked about, too, and as they both stood there the tick of the clock on the bedside table grew louder and louder, as if it were working hard to fill up a vacuum created by Chris's approaching absence.

"Chris," Cathy said, "Naomi's going to spend the night tonight, I told you. Do you mind if she sleeps in your room instead of in the guest room?"

"Why?" Chris cried.

"Oh, Chrissy, I'd much rather she slept in here!"

Chris shook her head in perplexity. "All right, but what I don't see is why a guest can't sleep in the guest room."

"Besides," Cathy threw in carelessly, "I'm not used to having this room empty. I can't stand having it empty. It gives me the creeps."

Cathy did not actually say she would miss her sister, and it had never entered Chris's head that she might. She gazed at Cathy in astonishment.

"Chris, you've got to get dressed," Cathy announced briskly. "It's two-thirty."

Now Chris had to hurry. Cathy helped by drawing her bath. She offered Chris her can of talcum powder to take. Chris put on clean clothes, and Cathy buttoned the soft white blouse while Chris zipped the plaid skirt. Chris was getting into her coat when Mother called, "It's time to go."

"I have to say good-by to my parakeet and Mr. Pickle and Fluff." Chris was breathless as she went downstairs, lugging the suitcase and Emily's umbrella. She made a kissing sound at the bird's cage and hugged the cats.

But at last she was climbing into the car with Mother and Jeff. Cathy dropped a hasty kiss on her forehead. "Have a super time, Chrissy."

"And have a good time at the movies and everything," Chris replied politely.

She waved and waved as the car went down the drive and turned onto the road, and Cathy, waving back, was lost to view.

They had quite a wait for the train. Mother said either her watch was fast or the train was late. But at last the warning bell set Chris's heart racing,

and the headlight of the engine came into view down the track. She kissed Mother and gave Jeff a hasty hug, so excited now that she scarcely knew what she was doing.

The conductor took her suitcase and helped her climb aboard. She turned to wave good-by to Mother and Jeff, then followed the conductor into the half-empty car. The train was moving. She was on her way.

The conductor stowed her suitcase on the rack, and Chris found her ticket for him to punch. "I'm going to Detroit." She simply couldn't help telling him.

"You're on the wrong train," he informed her gravely.

She laughed. "No, I'm not. My father is going to meet me in New York, and we're going to another station. I'm going on the Wolverine."

He joked with her for a moment, and left, and Chris slid along the seat to the window. It went through her mind briefly that she usually felt shy with strangers, but she had talked to the conductor with no effort at all. It was queer, but being by herself seemed to make her feel more courageous than when Cathy was along to take charge.

A stout woman joined her in the seat a few stops

farther on but, engrossed in her thoughts, Chris gazed out the window and scarcely noticed her.

The train rolled through the countryside. They stopped at stations. After a while the towns gave way to the Jersey meadows.

When they came to a halt again, Chris's thoughts had flown so far away that she did not even register the fact that the train was not at a station. It was some time, indeed, before she was really conscious they were at a standstill.

Then the woman beside her stirred impatiently and muttered. The train gave a jerk, moved a short distance, and came to a jolting halt again.

Chris looked up as the door of the car opened and the conductor came in and closed it behind him. He walked down the car to Chris's seat. "What time does your Detroit train leave?"

She told him.

He looked at his watch, put it away with a slight shake of his head, and went off. Chris began to feel uneasy. She wished they would get started. Finally the train did begin to move, slowly, with jerks. "We're almost half an hour late already," her seat companion complained, with a look at her wrist-watch.

"What time is it?" Chris asked.

"Twenty of six."

Twenty of six! Daddy had said he would meet her in New York at five fifteen. Real alarm began to rise in Chris. She slipped to the edge of her seat in a nervous effort to push the train along.

She was relieved when the conductor appeared again. He reached into the rack for her bag. "Come on, young lady," he said. "I'm going to take you as far forward as I can to save a couple of minutes when we get in."

Chris followed him. The train was rushing along now, and the conductor held her hand as they crossed one clattering, swaying vestibule after another until she could see only a baggage car ahead. "Sit in this front seat," the conductor said, "and be ready to hop out."

The train popped noisily out of daylight into the tunnel that stretched under the Hudson River. Chris sat clutching the arm of the seat with one hand, her suitcase with the other, as at last they emerged from the tunnel and felt their way with what seemed deliberately infuriating slowness into the great dim cavern of Pennsylvania Station.

She was the first one off the train. The conductor

put her bag into her hand, and she turned to start up the platform. And there, comforting sight, was Daddy, striding to meet her.

"What in the world happened?" He seized her bag and her hand. Chris had to run to keep up with his steps. "You're almost three quarters of an hour late!"

But he hardly listened to Chris's breathless explanation. The thing now was to get across the city.

This was the busiest hour of the day in New York. One taxi after another moved by, ignoring Daddy's signal. Then they caught a cab as it discharged a passenger, and Daddy put Chris in and climbed in after her. "Can you make Grand Central in fifteen minutes?" he asked the driver.

"I can try." The driver put down his flag and headed into the traffic.

Getting across New York at this hour was an obstacle race. Cars, buses, trucks, pedestrians, and traffic lights blocked their way. Starting, moving a few feet, stopping again, the taxi worked its way east, its meter ticking, its driver resigned. Daddy kept looking at his watch; Chris kept looking at Daddy's face for reassurance she did not get.

Now they were headed uptown, but the taxi crept. The driver uttered an exclamation and swung into a cross street, and for a few moments they covered ground. A red light held them up. They moved again.

When the cab stopped for another light Daddy reached into his pocket. "Let us out here," he told the driver. "We can make better time on foot." He thrust a bill into the man's hand.

Then they were on the sidewalk, and Chris was running to keep up. They were rushing along the street, escaping a red light, turning into another street. Chris panted and jogged along.

They were inside Grand Central Station and heading down the sloping ramp to the upper concourse. "My bag is checked," Daddy said. Chris saw the big clock in the middle of the station, and it said twenty-five minutes past six.

"That's the gate, right across there." Daddy pointed. "Go on and I'll come. Hurry."

The gate looked miles away across the station, and the concourse was crowded with people hurrying in all directions. Chris felt a sudden terror of being separated from her father in this vast, echoing, confusing place. She turned impulsively to follow him as he hurried away. Then she hesitated. She had a horrible thought. Suppose they missed the train? Would they have to go home, giving up the trip and walking in after all the excitement of leave-taking? She simply couldn't bear to do that!

And as she paused, the situation suddenly seemed familiar. How often she had held the school bus for Cathy! Forgetting everything but the need to get on the train, Chris started across the huge station at a determined run.

The trainman at the open gate looked at her questioningly. "My father's coming," she said.

He looked at his watch. "Father'd better hurry." Everybody looked at watches, Chris thought. Then she saw the big clock again, and the hand was moving toward six-thirty. The trainman put his hand on the gate.

"Oh, please don't let the train go!" Chris cried in agonized tones. Then she saw Daddy coming, heading for the gate on the run with their bags and his briefcase. "There he is!" she cried.

They slipped through the gate, which closed behind them with a clang of finality.

But they were still a long way from the train. Chris could hardly see it, far down the dim platform. Would it wait? She had no breath to waste in asking.

A conductor loomed up and came to meet them. "Better get on here, sir," he said.

They were on the train. A porter in a white coat had taken their luggage, and they were wending their way through the club car into a Pullman. This was a very different car from any Chris had ever seen. But she glanced out the broad window at one side of the narrow corridor, and she saw that the train was already moving, slipping silently, smoothly along the deserted platform.

CHAPTER EIGHT
A FRIEND FROM AWAY

"Right in here, sir," the porter said.

He had led Chris and her father past rows of tiny rooms, where people sat reading or looking out the window, and now they paused at one of the cubicles. "And roomette number six, directly across. Shall I put the young lady's suitcase in there, sir?"

"Please," Daddy said. "Are they serving dinner?"

"Yes, sir, dinner is being served. The dining car is just ahead."

"That's what we need." Daddy let out his breath in a long puff. "Well, Chris," he said, as the porter departed, "you've got something to tell the folks back home already. Get your breath and take off your hat and coat. And then let's eat."

A few minutes later they walked ahead through the car and across the vestibule, where the clack of the wheels on the rails, cushioned inside, grew loud and raucous. Ahead, Chris had a glimpse of white-covered tables, where already a few people were seated, and then her father opened the door into the dining car.

Nothing she had pictured had been half as exciting as this. A tantalizing aroma of charcoal-broiled steak filled the air. White-jacketed waiters hurried to and fro, trays held high on their lifted fingertips. The car was brightly lighted, and each table shone with starched linen and polished cutlery.

A smiling steward placed the Leonards at a table where Chris could sit next to the window and gaze out at the flying scene. The day was deepening toward dark, and lights shone from apartment houses on the fringe of the city. Soon the train was speeding through Westchester suburbs. Chris gazed, fascinated, at the well-kept houses and the small-town streets busy with cars until Daddy called her attention to the menu. "What would you like for dinner?"

She turned from the window to study the card, but her brow furrowed. When they ate at the

Copper Kettle she usually took what Cathy took. "I'll have what you have," she said.

"Why don't you decide for yourself?" Daddy asked. "You can read it, can't you?"

"Of course!" She looked up reprovingly.

"Then choose what you would like."

Chris went down the list slowly. Broiled fish, fried chicken, small sirloin steak. . . . "I'll have a small sirloin steak," she said.

She chose tomato juice, French fried potatoes, Russian dressing for her salad, and ice cream, and watched with interest as Daddy wrote the order on a slip of paper the steward had provided. The waiter brought them ice water and crisp rolls and butter, and scooped up the order. Chris watched him anxiously, but he seemed pleased with their selection as he hurried off.

She settled back with a sigh of relief after the ordeal of making up her mind. But she was starved, she realized, after eating almost nothing all day, and she had to begin devouring buttered rolls at once.

For the first time she had leisure to consider their almost missing the train. "What would we have done if we'd missed it?"

"We'd have stayed at a hotel and taken the first plane tomorrow."

So she would not have had to go home. But she was glad she was here, having dinner in this cozy, exciting, swaying dining car. "Wasn't it lucky I was used to holding the school bus, so I wasn't afraid to ask the man to hold the train!" Chris exclaimed.

"You held it," Daddy assured her. "The Wolverine was half a minute late pulling out, and I doubt if they'd have held it for anyone but a young lady wearing a round red hat."

She laughed delightedly. "Wait till I tell Cathy!" New assurance seemed to flow through her at the thought that they were on the train because she had held it.

Gazing out at the flying twilight scene, she tried to picture what was going on back in Middle Bridge. Cathy and Naomi were home from the movies by now. What were Jeff and Mother doing? But already the reality of home was dwindling, in proportion to the miles spinning out behind her. Reality was here and now, in this bright, swaying diner full of good smells and talking and people at dinner.

She devoured every bite of her meal. When she had scraped the ice-cream dish Daddy said, "Would you like to go back to the club car?"

The club car was like a living room, with armchairs and small tables along the sides. A man and woman were playing cards at one table, and Daddy said to Chris, "Would you care for a rollicking game of double solitaire?"

This seemed a happy idea and a porter brought them cards. Chris beat her father roundly. Two or three people stopped to look as they passed through and Chris began to feel as grown-up as anyone.

"Now are you ready for bed? We have to get up early," Daddy reminded her.

She was ready, not necessarily to go to sleep, but to realize at last the highlight of the trip—going to bed in a sleeping car. She led the way back to their car, then stood looking into her roomette with a frown. "But where do we sleep?"

Daddy reached up and grasped the top of the seat, pulling on it until a bed, tightly made up with sheets and tan blankets, detached itself from the wall and came down, filling the entire roomette. Chris gasped with surprise, then scrambled onto the bed.

"Now I'll unpack," she decided delightedly. "Where shall I put my things?"

Her father explained that one did not unpack in the cramped quarters of a Pullman, except for necessities. He pointed out the various convenient features of a roomette. Chris was enchanted. "You can turn out the top light and have just this little one on if you want to read. And if you turn out all the lights, you can pull the shade up and look out."

She undressed and brushed her teeth and got into bed, and Daddy came and kissed her good night. She had to experiment with the little handles that turned lights and air conditioning and a fan on and off. When she knew them, she turned off all but the little light over the head of the bed, and settled down with a book Cathy had slipped into her bag.

It was when she opened the book that she found the note, on Cathy's paper and in Cathy's writing. She opened the envelope wonderingly.

"Dear Chris," she read. "We are thinking of you. Have a wonderful time and come home soon. Happy birthday. Love and kisses." It was signed "Cathy," but Jeff had printed his name below hers. An unaccustomed warm and tender feeling swelled in Chris's heart. She read the note over several times, put it carefully back in its envelope, and replaced it in the book. It was a lovely surprise. After a moment she took it out of the book and slipped it gently under her pillow.

She decided not to read, after all, and turned out the light, sliding down between the smooth sheets with a sigh of peace. For a few minutes she listened to the rhythmic click and rattle of the wheels and felt the gentle shaking of her bed. Then Chris was asleep.

She woke up once in the night to feel the train motionless and to hear voices outside her window. Chris lifted herself on her elbow and raised the shade slightly. They were at a station, she saw, peeking out. She could see right into the lighted waiting room and ticket office, and on the platform two men wearing caps and holding long-spouted oil cans were chatting and laughing. My, but it was nice to be cozy here on the train and to be carried along! She snuggled down with an appreciative shiver of comfort, and felt the train lurch slightly as it moved.

Once more she awoke, as a pink dawn was streaking up from the horizon. They were speeding through farming country. She could see farms, much like the ones around Middle Bridge, and plain little houses still sleeping peacefully. No human beings were in sight, but tranquil cows gazed incuriously at the train from deep in the meadow grass. Through a small town the train rushed, and a bell, where the main street crossed the tracks, rose in pitch and fell again as they left it behind.

She planned to stay awake then, but roused to find Daddy shaking her gently. "We'll be in in an hour. Shall I push your bed up, so you can get dressed?"

She was glad of the sweater to slip quickly over her head. The tiny bowl, in which the water sloshed around with the movement of the train, she found rather unsatisfactory for washing, but Daddy told her she could wash at the hotel.

Then they made their way to the dining car again, where the steward knew them and conducted them to the same table. The car smelled of bacon this morning.

"Oh, can I write the order?" she begged. Daddy pushed the blank in front of her. She concentrated, writing her order and his with great care. She waited anxiously for the waiter's perusal, but he could read her writing and gave her a flashing smile.

She was beginning to feel very much at home in travel, and sipped her glass of ice water with composure, waiting for breakfast to come.

When they returned to their car the porter appeared, clothesbrush in hand. "Would the little lady like to have her coat brushed?"

Then Chris put on her hat and gloves, clutched her pocketbook and umbrella, and sat down to look out at the great city they were approaching. The train slowed, groped its way among switches, and pulled at last into the dim Detroit station.

The terminal was almost deserted, except for the stream of passengers moving off the Wolverine. Chris sat straight, her heart pounding, as their taxi headed out into the washed, early-morning streets, past parks and great buildings. They had quite a long ride before they pulled up in front of a hotel and a uniformed attendant opened the cab door.

The hotel, too, was almost deserted. Chris was awed by its elegance. Footsteps were soundless on the thick carpet, and the furniture and potted plants seemed most impressive. Then a boy was

carrying their bags and ushering them into an elevator, which moved upward so silently Chris was not certain they were moving at all.

Here was more carpet, and they were led down a long silent corridor lined with closed doors, except for one room where Chris glanced in to see a maid vacuuming the floor. Then she was in a bedroom, and the bellboy was opening a door into an adjoining room, where Daddy was to sleep, and raising windows and turning on lights. Finally he was gone, closing the door behind him. Chris drew a deep breath. She had arrived in Detroit.

She opened every drawer and read all the notices slipped under the glass top of her bureau. There was a telephone on a table beside the bed. From the window she could look far down on a busy street with traffic speeding along.

A bathroom, all white, gleaming tile, also adjoined the room. There were thick towels on the rack and cakes of soap in their wrappers. She examined the medicine chest, then hurried to her father's room. "I've got a whole bathroom. Is it just for me?"

"Just for you. I've got one too."

She had to peek into his bathroom to see if it

was like hers. This was luxury undreamed of. "I think I'll take a bath," Chris decided. "And I'll unpack my suitcase." Pleasant as it was to spend the night on a train, it was a relief to empty her bag and put it away in the spacious closet. She laid out her clothes carefully in a bureau drawer and hung up her coat and dress. The closet was so large it seemed a shame she had not brought more clothes with her.

Then Chris set the hot water thudding into the shiny tub and bathed lengthily and luxuriously. While she lay idling in the warm water she tried again to think of what they were doing at home now, but the images eluded her. It seemed so far away.

She had powdered herself liberally with Cathy's talcum and was getting into clean clothes when the phone rang, startling her. "Daddy, the telephone!" she called, almost in alarm.

"Answer it," he called back.

Chris raised the receiver timidly. "Hello?"

She was surprised to hear a girl's voice. "This is Mary Ellen Hammersmith."

That was the name of the man Daddy had come to see. "Oh, hello!" Chris said. "This is Chris Leonard," she added as an afterthought.

"Hello! My mother and I are down in the lobby. We came to get you to spend the day."

"Oh. Wait a minute, please." Excited, Chris turned to her father, standing in the door. "It's Mary Ellen Hammersmith. She's down in the lobby with her mother. They came to get me to spend the day."

"That's very nice," Daddy said. "Tell Mary Ellen that if they don't mind waiting a very few minutes we'll be down."

"If you don't mind waiting a very few minutes we'll be down. By." She hung up and began to fly into her new dress. She was beginning to feel tremendously important. Imagine! She could tell Cathy she not only had her own private bathroom, but her private phone too. She had had a telephone call herself, here in this strange city of Detroit, something she had almost never, in her whole life, had at home. Cathy had all the calls that were not for their parents.

And a girl named Mary Ellen Hammersmith was waiting for her in the lobby. She felt quite familiar with lobbies now. Yesterday she had barely heard the word.

They went down in the elevator, Daddy with his briefcase, Chris complete with hat, gloves, and bag, as this was Detroit. What did girls look like in Detroit, she wondered, as they dropped smoothly toward the lobby floor.

Mary Ellen and her mother rose to greet them. Mary Ellen seemed about her own age, brown-haired, pink-cheeked, and snub-nosed. She looked surprisingly like any girl in Middle Bridge. Her mother was a laughing young woman with whom Chris felt comfortable almost at once.

"We'll take good care of her," Mrs. Hammer-

smith promised Daddy. "We have various things planned, and tonight you are coming home with Rod to dinner."

Daddy was off in a taxi then, for his appointment with Mr. Hammersmith, and Chris followed Mary Ellen to the car. "You've had breakfast?" Mrs. Hammersmith inquired.

"We had it on the train. And dinner last night, too. In the dining car." She noticed that Mary Ellen wore neither hat nor gloves, and Chris took hers off and tossed them into the back seat. Now she felt much more like her usual self.

"Suppose we take you on a little tour of Detroit," Mrs. Hammersmith said.

They drove along the busy streets. Detroit looked to Chris as big as New York, and she leaned forward to gaze up at a tall building that Mary Ellen proudly pointed out. "It's almost as high as the Empire State Building," she told them politely.

They showed her great public buildings, and apartment houses so enormous they were practically cities in themselves. Chris could hardly believe those vast buildings, covering block after block and soaring into the sky, were places where people lived.

"Now let's take Chris to Greenfield Village," Mrs. Hammersmith said.

They saw a village copied from the past—a green with a general store, an inn, a school, a church. Chris gazed at a copy of the courthouse where Abraham Lincoln had practiced law. There were old homes, a mill, a post office.

They ate an early lunch in a charming restaurant. Back in Middle Bridge, Chris had worried about what she would say to a strange girl in Detroit, but now she found herself chattering. Mary Ellen had never been on a train overnight. Chris described her roomette, the diner, the club car.

They asked about her family. "Jeff is younger than me. Cathy's eleven, and she's very smart in school and can cook and everything," Chris told them.

"Too bad Cathy couldn't come too," Mrs. Hammersmith said.

"Oh," Chris explained quickly, "Cathy is very busy with her friends. She couldn't come to see me off, and she won't even be able to come with Jeff and Mother to meet me tomorrow." She paused. "She won't be home for my birthday dinner, either."

The Hammersmiths looked at her questioningly. "Tomorrow is my birthday," Chris explained. "Cathy was invited to a slumber party
at her friend Judy's. I don't mind." But she gazed
into space wistfully for a moment. "Nobody in
our family was ever away on a birthday before,"
she reflected.

"Well," Mary Ellen remarked, "my sister Stephanie is three. You'll see her. Sometimes she's a pest,
but she's cute. I adore her."

Her mother began to gather up her bag and
gloves. "Have we told Chris the plans for the
afternoon?"

"No." Mary Ellen shook her head. "Some
friends of mine are coming over to meet you."

"But first," her mother put in, "would you like
to drive over to Windsor?"

"Where's Windsor?"

"That's the town across the river in Canada."

"Canada's a foreign country!" Chris cried.

"That's right, it is." They both laughed in
sympathy at her excitement.

"I never thought I'd go to Canada!" Chris exclaimed in awe.

The tunnel to Windsor, under the Detroit

River, reminded her of the Lincoln Tunnel between New York and New Jersey. It was becoming apparent to Chris that one big city was much like another. She was beginning to take Detroit for granted.

When they emerged on the Windsor side, she looked about expectantly. "It doesn't look like a foreign country."

"Look up there." Mrs. Hammersmith pointed to a flag on a building. "There's the Union Jack."

True enough, the flag blowing in the breeze was not the familiar Stars and Stripes, and Chris felt a little thrill. This was proof she was in a foreign country! And a foreign country was something Cathy had never seen. She added the experience to the list of wonders she was treasuring.

A sign said, *Solicitor*. That was the British term for lawyer, Mrs. Hammersmith explained. In a shop window Chris and Mary Ellen spied a red-uniformed figure, a model of a Royal Northwest Mounted Policeman.

Going back to the tunnel, Mrs. Hammersmith become confused and stopped to consult a policeman. Chris listened to the brief conversation. "I could understand what he said!" she exclaimed, as they drove on.

Mary Ellen looked surprised. "Why shouldn't you?"

"This is a foreign country."

Her friends laughed, and Mary Ellen reminded her that Canada was closely related to England, and that English had been spoken in England before there had been a United States.

Chris was embarrassed at her mistake. But after a moment she giggled. "Silly me!" she said.

"Some time, Chris," Mrs. Hammersmith was saying, "come and spend your Easter vacation with Mary Ellen. We can show you lots of interesting things."

"Like the zoo!" Mary Ellen cried. "They don't have any cages for the animals. It's perfectly safe," she added quickly. "And, Chris, out in the country in the spring they grow millions of tulips!"

"I'd love to come." Chris sighed with contentment.

She sat quietly as they headed back to Detroit. This was a wonderful day. And Mary Ellen was one of the nicest girls she had ever met.

I really do have a new friend, Chris thought. A friend from away, too.

CHAPTER NINE
HAPPY BIRTHDAY

Mary Ellen Hammersmith's home was a modern ranch house. Chris gazed at it admiringly as they turned into the driveway. When they got out of the car, the front door opened, and a little girl ran to meet them.

"That's Stephie. Hi, Stephie," Mary Ellen called.

Stephie was a chubby child with a ponytail of straight dark hair, and she trotted after them when her sister said, "Come on into my room, Chris." Mary Ellen held out her hand to the little girl. "She's been with a sitter all day. Did you miss Mary Ellen, honey?" Stephie nodded gravely.

"I've got a little brother, Stephie," Chris said, "only he's older than you." Stephie shyly moved closer to Mary Ellen.

"I want to show you my dolls." Mary Ellen led the way into a charming bedroom with a chintz-covered bedspread and curtains to match. There was a dressing table with a full chintz skirt and a glass top.

"My sister has a dressing table," Chris remarked. For the first time it occurred to her that she would like one also. In fact, as she looked about at this pretty room, a desire stirred to go home and ask Mother if she could fix up her room like this and have some toilet water on the dressing table. She suddenly saw her room as she usually left it, with clothes strewn on chairs and shoes thrown hastily under the bed.

Mary Ellen's dolls sat in a row on a long window seat. "They're mostly all the ones I've ever had," she said. Stephie went off, and came back with a doll of her own to show Chris. Chris admired it extravagantly.

"Stephie," Mary Ellen said, "why don't you go and see what Mother is doing?"

"I want to stay here." Stephie was losing her shyness.

Mary Ellen sighed. "Then sit down quietly while I tell Chris about my dolls."

But Stephie could not sit quietly for long. She

knew all about the dolls, and she proceeded to assist Mary Ellen in relating the history of each. Finally Mary Ellen went out for a minute. "Mother wants you, Stephanie," she said, when she came back.

Stephanie showed no indication of hearing. It was only when her mother had called her twice that she finally picked up her own doll and dragged herself reluctantly from the room. Mary Ellen shook her head. "You don't know how much trouble it is, having a baby sister. Except, well, I really do adore her, only sometimes she's a nuisance. When my friends are here, she always wants to be where we are."

"I'm lucky mine's a boy," Chris replied. "Usually he doesn't bother Cathy and me too much."

Chris's eyes fell on a book lying on Mary Ellen's desk. She picked it up in amazement. "We have this reader in school!" she cried.

"You have?" Mary Ellen was astonished too, and for a while they pored over the pages so familiar to Chris, comparing their favorite stories and giggling at the funny parts.

"I can't get over it." Chris shook her head. "When I came to Detroit I thought it would be different, but you're just like girls at home, and we even have the same book!"

"I thought you'd be different, too," Mary Ellen confessed. "I never knew a girl from New York before."

"I don't live in New York. I live in Middle Bridge."

"But it's near New York."

Middle Bridge seemed to Chris a very long way from New York, but if Mary Ellen wanted to consider her "from New York" it was all right with her. It made her seem more—as Cathy would say —sophisticated. She rather liked being "from New York" when she was in Detroit.

She suddenly had an idea, an important idea. "Can you come to visit me some time, if your father has to come to New York?"

"I don't know. I'll ask."

"That would be super!" Chris cried. "Our house is bigger than yours, but it's older. Your bedroom is prettier than mine, too. I'm going to ask my mother if I can have a bedspread and curtains like yours. Cathy's room is all fixed up," she added. "She hounded my mother until she got it fixed up."

Mary Ellen cocked an ear. "There's the door-bell. That's Leslie and Frances."

They went to the door to meet Mary Ellen's friends. "Hi, Les. Hi, Frances," Mary Ellen greeted them. "This is Chris Leonard from New York. And guess what! She has the same reader we have."

"She does? Hi," Leslie said.

"Hi, Chris," said Frances. It was as if they were greeting a member of the same club.

"Hi," Chris returned, with hardly any feeling of shyness.

Leslie was dark and pretty. Frances had crinkly red hair and freckles, millions of freckles, on a very white skin. Chris studied their friendly faces and forgot they were strangers.

"What shall we play?" Mary Ellen inquired. "Shall we dress up?"

This, too, was like home, when Chris and Cathy, and sometimes Naomi, climbed to the attic and arrayed themselves in cast-off finery.

"The clothes are in our guest-room closet. Come on," Mary Ellen cried, leading the way.

They pulled out the clothes, and Chris gasped with admiration. There was a long, full black-tulle evening dress with a ruffled jacket over its low bodice. She appropriated that one immediately. Leslie found a flowered chiffon, Frances a rose-colored brocade. Stephie was in the midst of every-thing, dragging out one thing after another and finally pulling a bright red dress on over her feet.

Mary Ellen helped Chris slip the black dress over her head and zipped her up. "Oh, you look simply beautiful, Chris! Doesn't she, kids?"

They were too busy getting into their own togs to do more than glance her way, but Chris looked at herself in the mirror and felt a start of surprise. Why, she thought, I look pretty! When they dressed up at home it was Cathy who looked like a handsome and elegant lady, swishing around in the best of the old finery. Chris usually took what was left, fitting into it in any old fashion. It wasn't that Cathy was selfish; she just found what she wanted to wear more quickly than Chris.

"You ought always to wear black when you grow up, Chris." Mary Ellen was getting into a long, pleated white dress. "Stephie, you've got that on wrong. Come here."

Chris peeked once more at her flushed face and fair hair above the becoming black, and she sighed happily as she turned to rummage through a box of jewelry Mary Ellen had produced. I ought always to wear black. I ought always to wear black when I grow up. The phrase sang in her mind. She had always thought Cathy was pretty, but it had never occurred to her that she might be. The discovery somehow made her feel that she was Cathy's equal. It was a good, sound, satisfying feeling.

"Now my hat," Stephie was saying. "My hat, Mary Ellen!"

Mary Ellen brought it from a shelf and put it on her head. "You look darling, Stephie. Why don't you go out and show Mother?" she suggested craftily. Stephie simply ignored that suggestion. Obviously, here in the midst of all the fun was the place to be.

They staged a fashion show. They held contests, calling Mrs. Hammersmith in to choose the most beautiful, the silliest, the funniest, the prettiest, the weirdest, smartest, sweetest. Chris was chosen as the sweetest.

"Dearies, you'll have to excuse me," Mrs. Hammersmith declared at last. "I have business in the kitchen, and it concerns all of you."

They looked at one another knowingly. Refreshments, Chris thought, smiling at Leslie. She could smell something delicious. She was having a marvelous time. For almost the first time in her life, outside of school and an occasional party, she was part of a group her own age. She was accepted. She belonged. She was not here just because she was Cathy's little sister.

"Stephie's got to be the judge," Leslie said. Stephie sat on a chair in her red dress, hat askew, swinging her legs and pointing a plump finger at the winners. Chris laughed as hard as anyone when Stephie said she was the weirdest.

"She doesn't even know what that means," Mary Ellen said. "You silly goose, Stephie." She went over and bestowed a sound kiss on her little sister's cheek.

Mary Ellen's mother called her then, and while she was out of the room Leslie turned on the television and they all sat on the floor to watch cartoons.

"We have this program at home," Chris said. They giggled and commented companionably, Chris as much at home as the others.

Mary Ellen seemed to be gone a long time. But

at last she appeared at the door, looking mightily pleased. "Now will you all please come to the dining room."

They trooped out, but stopped with cries of surprise. The dining room was dark, and two tall white candles lighted the lace-covered table. Dishes of ice cream stood at five places. And as they stood there, the door from the kitchen opened and Mrs. Hammersmith came in, carrying a white-frosted cake ablaze with candles.

"Happy birthday to you," Mary Ellen and her mother began to sing, and the others joined in automatically, not knowing whose birthday they were celebrating. "Happy birthday to you. Happy birthday, dear Chrissy, happy birthday to you!"

"I didn't know it was your birthday," Leslie cried.

"Me either," said Frances.

"Neither did I," said Chris, and they all laughed. "I mean, I didn't know this was a birthday party."

"Chris's birthday is really tomorrow," Mrs. Hammersmith explained, "but we thought it would be fun to have a party today. Make a wish, Chris!"

Chris made some wish, but she was too flustered to remember later what she had wished for, and then she drew in her breath and blew a tremendous gust, and every candle went out.

It was when she picked up her napkin that she discovered presents. She looked up in confusion. "They're just little remembrances," Mrs. Hammersmith said.

"We didn't have any cards," Mary Ellen explained. "This one is from me, and this from Mother, and this from Stephie."

"This from me," Stephie repeated, reaching

over and dipping her sleeve into the ice cream.

"No fair, we didn't bring anything," Frances exclaimed.

There were a pretty handkerchief, a small bottle of toilet water, and a bright new pencil with a sharp point. Chris sniffed the toilet water over and over until Mary Ellen cried, "You'd better cut the cake, Chris, or we'll have ice-cream soup!"

"Ice-cream soup!" cried Stephie in delight, tipping over her glass of water. Her mother leaped for a towel. Mary Ellen pulled the startled child away from the table to save her from being soaked.

"I knew that would happen if she ate with us," Mary Ellen said, for the first time a trifle cross.

"It's only water." Her mother mopped matter-of-factly.

"Just like Jeff at our house," Chris said, shaking her head.

The cake and ice cream were eaten at last, and it was five-thirty, and more than time for the girls to go home.

"I hope you'll come again, Chris," Leslie said.

"I hope so too. We had the best time," Frances said enthusiastically.

Chris waved good-by to her new friends from

the door. She felt flushed with happiness and excitement and the unaccustomed fun of having friends.

Then they had to clear the party away and get dinner for Daddy and Mr. Hammersmith, who would be coming soon. Chris wiped dishes, chattering with Mary Ellen as if she had known her always. Potatoes were already baking, and Mrs. Hammersmith took a thick steak from the refrigerator.

The men came, and both girls rushed to meet them. "Daddy!" Chris cried. "Mary Ellen has the same reader I have. And some time when her father comes to New York on business she's coming to visit me!"

"Wonderful idea," said Daddy.

"Can I go some time?" Mary Ellen asked her father.

"We might be able to work it out," he told her.

Later Mr. Hammersmith drove them back to the hotel, Mary Ellen in the back seat with Chris. Chris was feeling real sorrow at the thought of leaving so soon this friend she had found. "I had a wonderful time. Thank you for the party and the presents and everything!"

"Oh, I had a wonderful time too. I hope you can come again soon."

"I will." Chris forgot how distant Detroit really was. It no longer seemed far away from Middle Bridge at all. "And you come and see me. Be sure."

"I will."

"O.K." She had to get out of the car. "By."

"By, Chris."

On the sidewalk Chris called, "Mary Ellen, write to me!"

"I will."

"I'll send you my address," Chris called back.

Just as the car was drawing away, she had another idea, the best one of all. She leaned into the car. "Mary Ellen," she cried, "when you come to visit me, we'll have a slumber party!"

CHAPTER TEN
ABOVE THE CLOUDS

Daddy pushed open the glass door of the hotel. "This is the best day of my whole life!" Chris told him, as they entered the lobby.

"I'm glad to hear that." He smiled down at her. "Look, the gift shop is still open. Would you like to buy something to take home?"

Chris gazed into the brightly lighted little emporium. "May I buy presents for Cathy and Jeff and Mother? I've got some money."

It took her a long time to decide, wandering along the shelves, while Daddy read his newspaper in the lobby. Finally Chris picked out a small pin for her mother, in the shape of a cat with topaz eyes, and some maple-sugar candy for Jeff. It was harder to find a present for Cathy, until she came

173

upon a small packet of spiced rose petals. She
bought two of them, so that she, too, could enjoy
the delightful fragrance among the things in her
bureau drawers. Her bureau drawers, she re-
solved, were going to be tidy and straight from
now on, to match her room.

She had another idea. It would be nice to take
presents to Janice and Emily. Once more she
slowly circled the shop, and found a folder of colored pictures of Detroit. She bought one of these
for herself, too, so she could point out to the family
all the sights she had seen. As she crossed the lobby
to her father, laden with purchases, a woman
smiled sympathetically. Chris beamed back.

They shot up to their floor in the elevator.
"How would you like to call home?" Daddy asked,
as he unlocked the door and switched on lights in
Chris's bedroom.

"Oh, yes! Can we? I want to tell Cathy about
Mary Ellen."

It took almost no time to get Mother on the
phone. After Daddy told her when their plane
would arrive, he handed the phone to Chris.
"Hello," she said, breathless. "Mother, I spent
the whole day with Mary Ellen. We went out to

lunch, and we went to her house, and she has twenty dolls. And I had a birthday cake. May I speak to Cathy?"

Cathy came on the line. "Cathy, I've got a surprise for you!" Chris cried, her eyes on the spiced rose petals on her bed.

"I've got one for you, too."

"You have?" Chris paused. There was so much to tell that she felt lost. "I have my own private bathroom," she announced. "And two of Mary Ellen's friends came, and we dressed up. May I speak to Jeff?"

But Jeff was in bed, and then Daddy said she had talked long enough. "Good-by for now," she said. "I'll see you tomorrow. I mean the next day," she corrected herself, remembering that Cathy would not be home.

She decided to take another bath, and she sang softly to herself as she lay back enjoying the warm water. "I'm going home tomorrow, I'm going home tomorrow. Tomorrow is my birthday," she sang on.

She had enjoyed every minute in Detroit, but Detroit was over now except for the novelty of sleeping in this unfamiliar bed in the high-up room looking down on the busy streets. And the plane trip home—she was looking forward to that.

The really big thrill ahead was seeing Mother and Cathy and Jeff again and telling them all about her trip. It seemed to her she had been away for weeks, she had so much to relate.

Chris reluctantly let the water out of the tub and helped herself to a thick, fresh bath towel. She scrubbed herself dry, applied a cloud of Cathy's powder, and slipped her nightgown over her head. Smelling of apple blossoms, she went in to kiss her father good night.

She stood at the window for a moment, then she climbed into bed. Why did strange beds feel so stiff? She turned on her side and was instantly asleep.

In the morning they had time for a leisurely breakfast in the cheerful hotel coffee shop. Chris drank icy orange juice and ate a slice of smoky-tasting ham, curling at the edges, with her egg.

Back in her room, she had to pack her suitcase again, rearranging the contents to make room for the newly acquired packages. She considered taking one more bath, but Daddy said it was unnecessary. He also discouraged her from taking home the unused cakes of soap. She could take the colored postcard showing the hotel. Chris carefully located on the card the window she thought was in her room, and put a circle around it.

Then, in midmorning, there was the taxi trip to the airport. And at last Chris was walking across the landing field and climbing steps into the plane. The interior of the airplane did not look strange to her, because it somewhat resembled a Pullman car, and she was familiar with Pullmans now.

Instead of a porter, however, a slim young lady, with gleaming pink-lacquered fingernails and wearing a smart uniform and cap, smiled and asked if she might take Chris's coat. Chris was used to having porters and waiters and bellboys, and people like that, do things for her now. She relinquished her coat and settled complacently into the window seat beside her father, as if flying were an old story.

She could see last-minute passengers scurrying across the field. The stewardess closed the door and Daddy fastened Chris's seat belt. Now the steps she had climbed were wheeled away. She felt the rumble of powerful engines.

They were moving slowly, pausing, moving again. Faster and faster. Sitting straight to look out the window, Chris saw the ground fall rapidly away and the horizon draw back until, in a few moments, she was looking down on a vast panorama of city countryside. Thrilled, her face close to the window, she strained to look down at the ground as the plane climbed higher and higher, until suddenly they were engulfed in clouds, like thick white fog, and she could see nothing.

With a little sigh, Chris leaned her head back against the seat. Now she had time to think about everything that had happened to her on the trip to Detroit. Beside her, Daddy was looking over some papers. Chris let her thoughts drift.

She found them dwelling especially on the events of yesterday. Such a long day. She traced it through breakfast in the dining car, their arrival at the hotel, Mary Ellen's phone call. Then the sight-seeing trip. Mary Ellen's house. Her thoughts arrived finally at Stephie.

Stephie is a sweet little girl, she thought, even though Mary Ellen does think she's a pest sometimes. Chris smiled to herself as she recalled Stephie's bland rejection of her sister's attempts to separate her from the big girls.

"Daddy?" She turned toward him.

"Yes, Chris?"

"Stephie—that's Mary Ellen's sister, you know—she's three. And she's so cute. But she kept coming into the room when Mary Ellen and I wanted to talk and read, and she was right in the middle of everything when we were all dressing up."

Daddy was smiling a little. "Just like you and Cathy?"

She looked up at him, surprised. "I don't ever. . . ." Then she turned away in confusion, feeling her face grow hot as the truth of Daddy's remark struck unexpectedly home.

Chris gazed out the window. Far below, through an opening in the clouds, she could glimpse a farm with its red barns and green fields. And with the same startling clarity, she could see herself making up excuses to ring Naomi's doorbell.

In sudden illumination, gazing down at the farm without seeing it, other things came back to Chris. Mary Ellen saying, "I really adore her. But when my friends are here, she always wants to be where we are." Like a distant echo, here was Cathy, patting her shoulder. "You're a nice girl, Chrissy, even if you are a pest sometimes." Cathy crying, "You always act hurt, and it's *frustrating!*"

Mary Ellen again. "You silly goose, Stephie," as she kissed her small sister. And Cathy, cross because she couldn't stand it to have Chris's room empty, telling her sister without meaning to that she was going to miss her. She thought of Stephie upsetting the water. Suddenly she saw herself dumping salad into Cathy's lap. Cathy had been very nice about it.

Chris thought of the letter Cathy had slipped into the book. She knew it by heart. "Dear Chris, We are thinking of you. Have a wonderful time and come home soon. Happy birthday. Love and kisses." Cathy's thoughts had been on the social events of her own vacation, yet she had taken the time to write that little message and slip it in where Chris would be sure to find it.

I always do want to be with her friends, Chris admitted in her heart. For a second she seemed to be gazing down on herself, just as she had looked down at small Stephie in the midst of the older girls. For the first time, she saw it from Cathy's viewpoint.

The clouds below the plane closed. And, like the glimpse of earth, Chris's moment of conscious insight passed somewhere deep into memory. She began to think about getting home.

I can't wait to see Janice, she thought, and give her the pictures of Detroit. Emily, too. She was looking forward eagerly to telling them all about her adventures. Both girls loomed importantly now as her friends.

If Mary Ellen comes to visit me some time, Chris thought, I really will have a slumber party, and invite Janice and Emily. I might even have some other friends by that time. Anyhow, I already have two friends at home and one from away. No, I have *three* friends away, she decided, Leslie and Frances too. Cathy only had Judy, she reflected. It was a marvelously satisfying feeling.

Chris's nose twitched as the smell of food assailed it, and she turned to look up the aisle. The stewardess appeared with a tray, which she presented to a passenger in a front seat. Chris realized she was hungry. "I didn't know you ate on planes," she told Daddy. This came as a delightful surprise. She watched, as one passenger after another was served, getting hungrier and hungrier and more and more curious as to what would be set before her.

Her turn came at last. A tray was slipped into a rack in front of her, another in front of Daddy. Chris lifted lids, examining each dish with relish.

There was fruit cup with a maraschino cherry in it. There were three luscious rolls of ham, surrounding fat stalks of asparagus. There was a salad. She found hot biscuits, cake, and milk. Sighing with contentment, Chris unfolded her napkin. Traveling was just lovely. She couldn't decide which was better—going to the dining car or having a tray brought right to her seat, like this.

She ate slowly, savoring each mouthful. This was one more thing with which to regale the family. How glad she was that she was the first one to take a trip, and could describe things to Cathy that Cathy, with all her sophistication, knew nothing about.

She gazed out the window as she ate. The patches of dark green below were mountains, Daddy said, although they did not look high from here. Then the stewardess was collecting the trays.

"We're almost in," Daddy said, consulting his watch.

Chris's heart began to flutter. Now it was Detroit that seemed remote and unreal. "Jeff will be here," she said. She was glad Jeff was coming to see her get off the plane. But it would have been perfect if Cathy could have come too.

A man's voice spoke through the loudspeaker. He was the captain, telling them how soon they would land at Newark and how long the flight had taken. When Chris looked out again they were below the clouds, and New York and its environs— one vast city as far as the eye could see—spread like magic beneath them.

The stewardess brought her coat. Chris reached for the train case and opened it to make sure the presents were safe. Now her seat belt was fastened again. They were dropping lower and lower, with the ground racing to meet them, and Chris had the same queer feeling in her stomach that riding in a fast elevator gave her. Then she felt a soft bump and a bounce, and the plane was skimming rapidly over the ground, slowing and stopping.

The door was open. The passengers lined up in the aisle. "Good-by, sir," the stewardess said to Daddy. She smiled at Chris. "Good-by, honey."

"Good-by. I had a very nice time," Chris said graciously.

She walked across the field sedately, as befitted a young lady traveler of experience, although she was conscious of the eyes she hoped were on her and anxiously searched the crowd waiting at the gate. As she neared the terminal, something began to jump up and down, and the something was Jeff. In spite of herself, Chris broke into a run.

"Chris!" Jeff was shouting. "I saw a whole enormous whale!"

"Well, I went to a foreign country." She kissed Mother. "Through a tunnel. And I. . . ."

Her words trailed off. From behind Mother, a broad smile on her face, Cathy suddenly appeared. Chris stopped, speechless.

"Oh, Chris," Cathy cried, laughing, "you looked so funny when you saw me!"

"But I thought. . . ." Then, suddenly, the fact that Cathy had come to meet her, after all, grew paramount, and why the plan for the slumber party at Judy's had been changed seemed unimportant right now. "Cathy," Chris cried, "we were on the fourteenth floor of the hotel, and I had a telephone beside my bed, and Mary Ellen called me up!"

"Lucky you," said Cathy.

Daddy had been kissed. They waited while he went to get his suitcase, which had been checked on the plane. Jeff wanted ice cream, and Mother went with him to get some.

"Cathy," Chris said, when they stood there

alone, her brow furrowing, "how come you didn't go to Judy's?"

"The party was changed to tomorrow. By the way, happy birthday, Chris. Want me to carry your bag?"

Chris handed it over absent-mindedly. "Why was it changed?"

"Well," Cathy said, "remember one day I told you I had an idea, only wild horses wouldn't drag it out of me?"

"Yes."

"That was when I decided I'd ask Judy if she could change the party to tomorrow, if it was convenient for everyone. And it was. So she did."

Chris was still puzzled. "Just on account of me?"

"Oh—I like meat loaf," Cathy said lightly.

And suddenly they were laughing and laughing together, unconscious of the people around them. Chris laughed, because now she knew, without Cathy's saying so, that her sister had wanted all along to be here for the fun of her homecoming and the birthday dinner. Cathy laughed because Chris laughed, and because she was happy to be here.

"Oh, Chris, you're so silly!" Cathy gasped, wiping her eyes.

"So are you!" Chris retorted.

Daddy and Mother and Jeff were all coming back, and the group began to walk toward the parking lot. "By the way," Cathy was saying, "Gretchen's having a cookout Saturday. You're invited, too."

"I am?"

This was a pleasant surprise. But, inexplicably, Stephie came into Chris's mind, Stephie in the midst of the bigger girls. "I may not go," she said suddenly. "I have a lot of things to do. I want to write a letter to my friend in Detroit. . . ."

She glanced at Cathy, and was rewarded by a look of astonishment on her sister's face. It occurred to Chris that of course Cathy had supposed she would jump at the chance to go to a cookout with the bigger girls. Now that she thought about it, Chris was rather surprised herself. Somehow she felt older and more sophisticated than Cathy.

She turned to her mother. "May I have Janice over tomorrow? I brought her something."

"That would be nice." Mother smiled.

Jeff was shouting. "I saw the hugest dinosaur bones, Chris!"

"And I slept in this bed that folded up, on the train," Chris related.

"Oh, Chris, that movie was really terrific," Cathy cried. "There was this girl. . . ."

They were crossing the parking lot, Chris, Cathy, and Jeff marching abreast.

"I went to the zoo and saw the seal do tricks," Jeff was shouting.

"You did! Cathy, I have three new friends in Detroit."

"That's nice. There was this goofy girl in the picture, Chris. . . ."

Chris spied the car. She was glad to see it, it meant they would soon be home. And so many lovely things lay ahead of her there. Her birthday dinner, with the whole family home the way they always were on birthdays. And her birthday presents. She had the gifts from Detroit to distribute, too. And the long delicious story of her adventures to tell everyone.

Tomorrow, while Cathy was away, she would ask Janice over. With sudden daring inspiration she thought, maybe she could spend the night!

She had to write to Mary Ellen, so Mary Ellen could write back. Then I want to discuss my room with Mother, she thought, and start getting it fixed up, like Cathy's and Mary Ellen's. Oh, she had so much to do!

"Wasn't that a scream, Chris?" Cathy was demanding.

"Yes!" Chris agreed, laughing obligingly, though she hadn't heard a word of what Cathy had said.

She gave a skip of happiness and anticipation. Unconsciously, she was leading the way now. Cathy and Jeff, both talking at once, followed her to the car.

Though she was born in Chicago, Catherine Woolley has lived almost all her life in Passaic, New Jersey, where she is well known for her community activities.

A former member of the Passaic Board of Education, she has been active on many local citizens' committees. She has served on the Passaic Redevelopment Agency, is a member of the board of directors and past president of the League of Women Voters of Passaic, a member of the Red Cross Motor Corps, and on the board of directors of the Passaic-Clifton Young Women's Christian Association. Miss Woolley owns an old house in Truro, on Cape Cod, and she spends a good part of every year there.

After graduating from the University of California at Los Angeles, she returned to New York City, where she was in advertising, public relations, and editorial work until 1947. Her interest in her own young nephews and nieces drew her to the field of writing for children, and her first book for William Morrow and Company, *Two Hundred Pennies,* was published in 1947.

Since then Catherine Woolley has become widely known for her stories. In addition, she has gained a large following for her picture books, which she writes under the pen name of Jane Thayer. Her stories also appear in children's magazines and are included in many juvenile anthologies.